SKETCHES IN LAVENDER
BLUE AND GREEN

SKETCHES IN LAVENDER BLUE AND GREEN

JEROME K. JEROME

WILDSIDE PRESS

SKETCHES IN LAVENDER BLUE AND GREEN

Copyright ©

Published in 2007 by Wildside Press.
www.wildsidepress.com

CONTENTS

La-ven-der's blue, did-dle, did-dle!
La-ven-der's green;
When I am king, did-dle, did-dle!
You shall be queen.
Call up your men, did-dle, did-dle!
Set them to work;
Some to the plough, did-dle, did-dle!
Some to the cart.
Some to make hay, did-dle, did-dle!
Some to cut corn;
While you and I, did-dle, did-dle!
Keep ourselves warm.

REGINALD BLAKE, FINANCIER AND CAD

The advantage of literature over life is that its characters are clearly defined, and act consistently. Nature, always inartistic, takes pleasure in creating the impossible. Reginald Blake was as typical a specimen of the well-bred cad as one could hope to find between Piccadilly Circus and Hyde Park Corner. Vicious without passion, and possessing brain without mind, existence presented to him no difficulties, while his pleasures brought him no pains. His morality was bounded by the doctor on the one side, and the magistrate on the other. Careful never to outrage the decrees of either, he was at forty-five still healthy, though stout; and had achieved the not too easy task of amassing a fortune while avoiding all risk of Holloway. He and his wife, Edith (*née* Eppington), were as ill-matched a couple as could be conceived by any dramatist seeking material for a problem play. As they stood before the altar on their wedding morn, they might have been taken as symbolising satyr and saint. More than twenty years his junior, beautiful with the beauty of a Raphael's Madonna, his every touch of her seemed a sacrilege. Yet once in his life Mr. Blake played the part of a great gentleman; Mrs. Blake, on the same occasion, contenting herself with a singularly mean *rôle* — mean even for a woman in love.

The affair, of course, had been a marriage of convenience. Blake, to do him justice, had made no pretence to anything beyond admiration and regard. Few things grow monotonous sooner than irregularity. He would tickle his jaded palate with respectability, and try for a change the companionship of a good woman. The girl's face drew him, as the moonlight holds a man who, bored by the noise, turns from a heated room to press his forehead to the window-pane. Accustomed to bid for what he wanted, he offered his price. The Eppington family was poor and numerous. The girl, bred up to the false notions of duty inculcated by a narrow conventionality, and, feminine like, half in love with martyrdom for its own sake, let her father bargain for a higher price, and then sold herself.

To a drama of this description, a lover is necessary, if the complications are to be of interest to the outside world. Harry Sennett, a pleasant-looking enough young fellow, in spite of his receding chin, was possessed, perhaps, of more good intention than sense. Under the influence of Edith's stronger character he was soon persuaded to acquiesce meekly in the proposed arrangement. Both succeeded in convincing themselves that they were acting nobly. The tone of the farewell interview, arranged for the eve of the wedding, would have been fit and proper to the occasion had Edith been a modern Joan of Arc about to sacrifice her own happiness on the altar of a great cause; as the girl was merely selling herself into ease and luxury, for no higher motive than the desire to enable a certain number of more or less worthy relatives to continue living beyond their legitimate means, the sentiment was perhaps exaggerated. Many tears were shed, and many everlasting good-byes spoken, though, seeing that Edith's new home would be only a few streets off, and that of necessity their social set would continue to be the same, more experienced persons might have counselled hope. Three months after the marriage they found themselves side by side at the same dinner-table; and after a little melodramatic fencing with what they were pleased to regard as fate, they accommodated themselves to the customary positions.

Blake was quite aware that Sennett had been Edith's lover. So had half a dozen other men, some younger, some older than himself. He felt no more embarrassment at meeting them than, standing on the pavement outside the Stock Exchange, he would have experienced greeting his brother jobbers after a settling day that had transferred a fortune from their hands into his. Sennett, in particular, he liked and encouraged. Our whole social system, always a mystery to the philosopher, owes its existence to the fact that few men and women possess sufficient intelligence to be interesting to themselves. Blake liked company, but not much company liked Blake. Young Sennett, however, could always be relied upon to break the tediousness of the domestic dialogue. A common love of sport drew the two men together. Most of us improve upon closer knowledge, and so they came to find good in one another.

"That is the man you ought to have married," said Blake one night to his wife, half laughingly, half seriously, as they sat alone, listening to Sennett's departing footsteps echoing upon the deserted pavement. "He's a good fellow — not a mere money-grubbing machine like me."

And a week later Sennett, sitting alone with Edith, suddenly broke out with:

"He's a better man than I am, with all my high-falutin' talk, and, upon my soul, he loves you. Shall I go abroad?"

"If you like," was the answer.

"What would you do?"

"Kill myself," replied the other, with a laugh, "or run away with the first man that asked me."

So Sennett stayed on.

Blake himself had made the path easy to them. There was little need for either fear or caution. Indeed, their safest course lay in recklessness, and they took it. To Sennett the house was always open. It was Blake himself who, when unable to accompany his wife, would suggest Sennett as a substitute. Club friends shrugged their shoulders. Was the man completely under his wife's thumb; or, tired of her, was he playing some devil's game of his own? To most of his acquaintances the latter explanation seemed the more plausible.

The gossip, in due course, reached the parental home. Mrs. Eppington shook the vials of her wrath over the head of her son-in-law. The father, always a cautious man, felt inclined to blame his child for her want of prudence.

"She'll ruin everything," he said. "Why the devil can't she be careful?"

"I believe the man is deliberately plotting to get rid of her," said Mrs. Eppington. "I shall tell him plainly what I think."

"You're a fool, Hannah," replied her husband, allowing himself the licence of the domestic hearth. "If you are right, you will only precipitate matters; if you are wrong, you will tell him what there is no need for him to know. Leave the matter to me. I can sound him without giving anything away, and meanwhile you talk to Edith."

So matters were arranged, but the interview between mother and daughter hardly improved the position. Mrs. Eppington was conventionally moral; Edith had been thinking for herself, and thinking in a bad atmosphere. Mrs. Eppington, grew angry at the girl's callousness.

"Have you no sense of shame?" she cried.

"I had once," was Edith's reply, "before I came to live here. Do you know what this house is for me, with its gilded mirrors, its couches, its soft carpets? Do you know what I am, and have been for two years?"

The elder woman rose, with a frightened pleading look upon her face, and the other stopped and turned away towards the window.

"We all thought it for the best," continued Mrs. Eppington meekly.

The girl spoke wearily without looking round.

"Oh! every silly thing that was ever done, was done for the best. *I* thought it would be for the best, myself. Everything would be so simple if only we were not alive. Don't let's talk any more. All you can say is quite right."

The silence continued for a while, the Dresden-china clock on the mantelpiece ticking louder and louder as if to say, "I, Time, am here. Do not make your plans forgetting me, little mortals; I change your thoughts and wills. You are but my puppets."

"Then what do you intend to do?" demanded Mrs. Eppington at length.

"Intend! Oh, the right thing of course. We all intend that. I shall send Harry away with a few well-chosen words of farewell, learn to love my husband and settle down to a life of quiet domestic bliss. Oh, it's easy enough to intend!"

The girl's face wrinkled with a laugh that aged her. In that moment it was a hard, evil face, and with a pang the elder woman thought of that other face, so like, yet so unlike — the sweet pure face of a girl that had given to a sordid home its one touch of nobility. As under the lightning's flash we see the whole arc of the horizon, so Mrs. Eppington looked and saw her child's life. The gilded, over-furnished room vanished. She and a big-eyed, fair-haired child, the only one of her children she had ever understood, were playing wonderful games in the twilight among the shadows of a tiny attic. Now she was the wolf, devouring Edith, who was Red Riding Hood, with kisses. Now Cinderella's prince, now both her wicked sisters. But in the favourite game of all, Mrs. Eppington was a beautiful princess, bewitched by a wicked dragon, so that she seemed to be an old, worn woman. But curly-headed Edith fought the dragon, represented by the three-legged rocking-horse, and slew him with much shouting and the toasting-fork. Then Mrs. Eppington became again a beautiful princess, and went away with Edith back to her own people.

In this twilight hour the misbehaviour of the "General," the importunity of the family butcher, and the airs assumed by cousin Jane, who kept two servants, were forgotten.

The games ended. The little curly head would be laid against her breast "for five minutes' love," while the restless little brain framed the endless question that children are for ever asking in all its thousand forms, "What is life, mother? I am very little, and I think, and think, until I grow frightened. Oh, mother, tell me, what is life?"

Had she dealt with these questions wisely? Might it not have been better to have treated them more seriously? Could life after all be ruled by maxims learned from copy-books? She had answered as she had been answered in her own far-back days of questioning. Might it not have been better had she thought for herself?

Suddenly Edith was kneeling on the floor beside her.

"I will try to be good, mother."

It was the old baby cry, the cry of us all, children that we are, till mother Nature kisses us and bids us go to sleep.

Their arms were round each other now, and so they sat, mother and child once more. And the twilight of the old attic, creeping westward from the east, found them again.

The masculine duet had more result, but was not conducted with the *finesse* that Mr. Eppington, who prided himself on his diplomacy, had intended. Indeed, so evidently ill at ease was that gentleman, when the moment came for talk, and so palpably were his pointless remarks mere efforts to delay an unpleasant subject, that Blake, always direct bluntly though not ill-naturedly asked him, "How much?"

Mr. Eppington was disconcerted.

"It's not that — at least that's not what I have come about," he answered confusedly.

"What have you come about?"

Inwardly Mr. Eppington cursed himself for a fool, for the which he was perhaps not altogether without excuse. He had meant to act the part of a clever counsel, acquiring information while giving none; by a blunder, he found himself in the witness-box.

"Oh, nothing, nothing," was the feeble response, "merely looked in to see how Edith was."

"Much the same as at dinner last night, when you were here," answered Blake. "Come, out with it."

It seemed the best course now, and Mr. Eppington took the plunge.

"Don't you think," he said, unconsciously glancing round the room to be sure they were alone, "that young Sennett is a little too much about the house?"

Blake stared at him.

"Of course, we know it is all right — as nice a young fellow as ever lived — and Edith — and all that. Of course, it's absurd, but —"

"But what?"

"Well, people will talk."

"What do they say?"

The other shrugged his shoulders.

Blake rose. He had an ugly look when angry, and his language was apt to be coarse.

"Tell them to mind their own business, and leave me and my wife alone." That was the sense of what he said; he expressed himself at greater length, and in stronger language.

"But, my dear Blake," urged Mr. Eppington, "for your own sake, is it wise? There was a sort of boy and girl attachment between them — nothing of any moment, but all that gives colour to gossip. Forgive me, but I am her father; I do not like to hear my child talked about."

"Then don't open your ears to the chatter of a pack of fools," replied his son-in-law roughly. But the next instant a softer expression passed over his face, and he laid his hand on the older man's arm.

"Perhaps there are many more, but there's one good woman in the world," he said, "and that's your daughter. Come and tell me that the Bank of England is getting shaky on its legs, and I'll listen to you."

But the stronger the faith, the deeper strike the roots of suspicion. Blake said no further word on the subject, and Sennett was as welcome as before. But Edith, looking up suddenly, would sometimes find her husband's eyes fixed on her with a troubled look as of some dumb creature trying to understand; and often he would slip out of the house of an evening by himself, returning home hours afterwards, tired and mud-stained.

He made attempts to show his affection. This was the most fatal thing he could have done. Ill-temper, ill-treatment even, she might have borne. His clumsy caresses, his foolish, halting words of tenderness became a horror to her. She wondered whether to laugh or to strike at his upturned face. His tactless devotion filled her life as with some sickly perfume, stifling her. If only she could be by herself for a little while to think! But he was with her night and day. There were times when, as he would cross the room towards her, he grew monstrous until he towered above her, a formless thing such as children dream of. And she would sit with her lips tight pressed, clutching the chair lest she should start up screaming.

Her only thought was to escape from him. One day she hastily packed a few necessaries in a small hand-bag and crept unperceived from the house. She drove to Charing Cross, but the Continental Express did not leave for an hour, and she had time to think.

Of what use was it? Her slender stock of money would soon be gone; how could she live? He would find her and follow her. It was all so hopeless!

Suddenly a fierce desire of life seized hold of her, the angry answer of her young blood to despair. Why should she die, never having known what it was to live? Why should she prostrate herself before this juggernaut of other people's respectability? Joy called to her; only her own cowardice stayed her from stretching forth her hand and gathering it. She returned home a different woman, for hope had come to her.

A week later the butler entered the dining room, and handed Blake a letter addressed to him in his wife's handwriting. He took it without a word, as though he had been expecting it. It simply told him that she had left him for ever.

The world is small, and money commands many services. Sennett had gone out for a stroll; Edith was left in the tiny *salon* of their *appartement* at Fécamp. It was the third day of their arrival in the town. The door was opened and closed, and Blake stood before her.

She rose frightened, but by a motion he reassured her. There was a quiet dignity about the man that was strange to her.

"Why have you followed me?" she asked.

"I want you to return home."

"Home!" she cried. "You must be mad. Do you not know —"

He interrupted her vehemently. "I know nothing. I wish to know nothing. Go back to London at once. I have made everything right; no one suspects. I shall not be there; you will never see me again, and you will have an opportunity of undoing your mistake — our mistake."

She listened. Hers was not a great nature, and the desire to obtain happiness without paying the price was strong upon her. As for his good name, what could that matter? he urged. People would only say that he had gone back to the evil from which he had emerged, and few would be surprised. His life would go on much as it had done, and she would only be pitied.

She quite understood his plan; it seemed mean of her to accept his proposal, and she argued feebly against it. But he overcame all her objections. For his own sake, he told her, he would prefer the scandal to be connected with his name rather than with that of his wife. As he unfolded his scheme, she began to feel that in acquiescing she was conferring a favour. It was not the first deception he had arranged for the public, and he appeared to be half in love with his own cleverness. She even found herself laughing at his mimicry of what this acquaintance and that would say. Her spirits rose; the play that might have been a painful drama seemed turning out an amusing farce.

The thing settled, he rose to go, and held out his hand. As she looked up into his face, something about the line of his lips smote upon her.

"You will be well rid of me," she said. "I have brought you nothing but trouble."

"Oh, trouble," he answered. "If that were all! A man can bear trouble."

"What else?" she asked.

His eyes travelled aimlessly about the room. "They taught me a lot of things when I was a boy," he said, "my mother and others — they meant well — which as I grew older I discovered to be lies; and so I came to think that nothing good was true, and that everything and everybody was evil. And then —"

His wandering eyes came round to her and he broke off abruptly. "Good-bye," he said, and the next moment he was gone.

She sat wondering for a while what he had meant. Then Sennett returned, and the words went out of her head.

A good deal of sympathy was felt for Mrs. Blake. The man had a charming wife; he might have kept straight; but as his friends added, "Blake always was a cad."

AN ITEM OF FASHIONABLE INTELLIGENCE

Speaking personally, I do not like the Countess of —-. She is not the type of woman I could love. I hesitate the less giving expression to this sentiment by reason of the conviction that the Countess of —- would not be unduly depressed even were the fact to reach her ears. I cannot conceive the Countess of —-'s being troubled by the opinion concerning her of any being, human or divine, other than the Countess of —-.

But to be honest, I must admit that for the Earl of —- she makes an ideal wife. She rules him as she rules all others, relations and retainers, from the curate to the dowager, but the rod, though firmly held, is wielded with justice and kindly intent. Nor is it possible to imagine the Earl of —-'s living as contentedly as he does with any partner of a less dominating turn of mind. He is one of those weak-headed, strong-limbed, good-natured, childish men, born to be guided in all matters, from the tying of a neck-cloth to the choice of a political party, by their women folk. Such men are in clover when their proprietor happens to be a good and sensible woman, but are to be pitied when they get into the hands of the selfish or the foolish. As very young men, they too often fall victims to bad-tempered chorus girls or to middle-aged matrons of the class from which Pope judged all womankind. They make capital husbands when well managed; treated badly, they say little, but set to work, after the manner of a dissatisfied cat, to find a kinder mistress, generally succeeding. The Earl of —- adored his wife, deeming himself the most fortunate of husbands, and better testimonial than such no wife should hope for. Till the day she snatched him away from all other competitors, and claimed him for her own, he had obeyed his mother with a dutifulness bordering on folly. Were the countess to die to-morrow, he would be unable to tell you his mind on any single subject until his eldest daughter and his still unmarried sister, ladies both of strong character, attracted towards one another by a mutual antagonism, had settled between themselves which was to be mistress of him and of his house.

However, there is little fear (bar accidents) but that my friend the countess will continue to direct the hereditary vote of the Earl of —- towards the goal of common sense and public good, guide his social policy with judgment and kindness, and manage his estates with prudence and economy for many years to come. She is a hearty, vigorous lady, of generous proportions, with the blood of sturdy forebears in her veins, and one who takes the same excellent good care of herself that she bestows on all others dependent upon her guidance.

"I remember," said the doctor — we were dining with the doctor in homely fashion, and our wives had adjourned to the drawing-room to discuss servants and husbands and other domestic matters with greater freedom, leaving us to the claret and the twilight — "I remember when we had the cholera in the village — it must be twenty years ago now — that woman gave up the London season to stay down here and take the whole burden of the trouble upon her own shoulders. I do not feel any call to praise her; she liked the work, and she was in her element, but it was good work for all that. She had no fear. She would carry the children in her arms if time pressed and the little ambulance was not at hand. I have known her sit all night in a room not twelve feet square, between a dying man and his dying wife. But the thing never touched her. Six years ago we had the small-pox, and she went all through that in just the same way. I don't believe she has ever had a day's illness in her life. She will be physicking this parish when my bones are rattling in my coffin, and she will be laying down the laws of literature long after your statue has become a familiar ornament of Westminster Abbey. She's a wonderful woman, but a trifle masterful."

He laughed, but I detected a touch of irritation in his voice. My host looked a man wishful to be masterful himself. I do not think he quite relished the calm way in which this grand dame took possession of all things around her, himself and his work included.

"Did you ever hear the story of the marriage?" he asked.

"No," I replied, "whose marriage? The earl's?"

"I should call it the countess's," he answered. "It was the gossip of the county when I first came here, but other curious things have happened among us to push it gradually out of memory. Most people, I really believe, have quite forgotten that the Countess of —- once served behind a baker's counter."

"You don't say so," I exclaimed. The remark, I admit, sounds weak when written down; the most natural remarks always do.

"It's a fact," said the doctor, "though she does not suggest the shop-girl, does she? But then I have known countesses, descended in a direct line from William the Conqueror, who did, so things balance one another. Mary, Countess of —-, was, thirty years ago, Mary Sewell, daughter of a Taunton linen-draper. The business, profitable enough as country businesses go, was inadequate for the needs of the Sewell family, consisting, as I believe it did, of seven boys and eight girls. Mary, the youngest, as soon as her brief schooling was over, had to shift for herself. She seems to have tried her hand at one or two things, finally taking service with a cousin, a baker and confectioner, who was doing well in Oxford Street. She must have been a remarkably attractive girl; she's a handsome woman now. I can picture that soft creamy skin when it was fresh and smooth, and the West of England girls run naturally to dimples and eyes that glisten as though they had been just washed in morning dew. The shop did a good trade in ladies' lunches — it was the glass of sherry and sweet biscuit period. I expect they dressed her in some neat-fitting grey or black dress, with short sleeves, showing her plump arms, and that she flitted around the marble-topped tables, smiling, and looking cool and sweet. There the present Earl of —-, then young Lord C—-, fresh from Oxford, and new to the dangers of London bachelordom, first saw her. He had accompanied some female relatives to the photographer's, and, hotels and restaurants being deemed impossible in those days for ladies, had taken them to Sewell's to lunch. Mary Sewell waited upon the party; and now as many of that party as are above ground wait upon Mary Sewell."

"He showed good sense in marrying her," I said, "I admire him for it." The doctor's sixty-four Lafitte was excellent. I felt charitably inclined towards all men and women, even towards earls and countesses.

"I don't think he had much to do with it," laughed the doctor, "beyond being, like Barkis, 'willing.' It's a queer story; some people profess not to believe it, but those who know her ladyship best think it is just the story that must be true, because it is so characteristic of her. And besides, I happen to know that it is true."

"I should like to hear it," I said.

"I am going to tell it you," said the doctor, lighting a fresh cigar, and pushing the box towards me.

I will leave you to imagine the lad's suddenly developed appetite for decantered sherry at sixpence a glass, and the familiar currant bun of our youth. He lunched at Sewell's shop, he tea'd at Sewell's, occasionally he dined at Sewell's, off cutlets, followed by assorted pastry. Possibly, merely from fear lest the affair should reach his mother's ears, for he was neither worldly-wise nor vicious, he made love to Mary under an assumed name; and to do the girl justice, it must be remembered that she fell in love with and agreed to marry plain Mr. John Robinson, son of a colonial merchant, a gentleman, as she must have seen, and a young man of easy means, but of a position not so very much superior to her own. The first intimation she received that her lover was none other than Lord C——, the future Earl of ——, was vouchsafed her during a painful interview with his lordship's mother.

"I never knew it, madam," asserted Mary, standing by the window of the drawing-room above the shop, "upon my word of honour, I never knew it"

"Perhaps not," answered her ladyship coldly. "Would you have refused him if you had?"

"I cannot tell," was the girl's answer; "it would have been different from the beginning. He courted me and asked me to be his wife."

"We won't go into all that," interrupted the other; "I am not here to defend him. I do not say he acted well. The question is, how much will compensate you for your natural disappointment?"

Her ladyship prided herself upon her bluntness and practicability. As she spoke she took her cheque-book out of her reticule, and, opening it, dipped her pen into the ink. I am inclined to think that the flutter of that cheque-book was her ladyship's mistake. The girl had common sense, and must have seen the difficulties in the way of a marriage between the heir to an earldom and a linen-draper's daughter; and had the old lady been a person of discernment, the interview might have ended more to her satisfaction. She made the error of judging the world by one standard, forgetting there are individualities. Mary Sewell came from a West of England stock that, in the days of Drake and Frobisher, had given more than one able-bodied pirate to the service of the country, and that insult of the cheque-book put the fight into her. Her lips closed with a little snap, and the fear fell from her.

"I am sorry I don't see my way to obliging your ladyship," she said.

"What do you mean, girl?" asked the elder woman.

"I don't mean to be disappointed," answered the girl, but she spoke quietly and respectfully. "We have pledged our word to one another. If he is a gentleman, as I know he is, he will keep his, and I shall keep mine."

Then her ladyship began to talk reason, as people do when it is too late. She pointed out to the girl the difference of social position, and explained to her the miseries that come from marrying out of one's station. But the girl by this time had got over her surprise, and perhaps had begun to reflect that, in any case, a countess-ship was worth fighting for. The best of women are influenced by such considerations.

"I am not a lady, I know," she replied quietly, "but my people have always been honest folk, well known, and I shall try to learn. I am not wishing to speak disrespectfully of my betters, but I was in service before I came here, ma'am, as lady's maid, in a place where I saw much of what is called Society. I think I can be as good a lady as some I know, if not better."

The countess began to grow angry again. "And who do you think will receive you?" she cried, "a girl who has served in a pastry-cook's shop!"

"Lady L—- came from behind the bar," Mary answered, "and that's not much better. And the Duchess of C—-, I have heard, was a ballet girl, but nobody seems to remember it. I don't think the people whose opinion is worth having will object to me for very long." The girl was beginning rather to enjoy the contest.

"You profess to love my son," cried the countess fiercely, "and you are going to ruin his life. You will drag him down to your own level."

The girl must have looked rather fine at that moment, I should dearly love to have been present.

"There will be no dragging down, my lady," she replied, "on either side. I do love your son very dearly. He is one of the kindest and best of gentlemen. But I am not blind, and whatever amount of cleverness there may be between us belongs chiefly to me. I shall make it my duty to fit myself for the position of his wife, and to help him in his work. You need not fear, my lady, I shall be a good wife to him, and he shall never regret it. You might find him a richer wife, a better educated wife, but you will never find him a wife who will be more devoted to him and to his interests."

That practically brought the scene to a close. The countess had sense enough to see that she was only losing ground by argument. She rose and replaced her cheque-book in her bag.

"I think, my good girl, you must be mad," she said; "if you will not allow me to do anything for you, there's an end to the matter. I did not come here to quarrel with you. My son knows his duty to me and to his family. You must take your own course, and I must take mine."

"Very well, my lady," said Mary Sewell, holding the door open for her ladyship to pass out, "we shall see who wins."

But however brave a front Mary Sewell may have maintained before the enemy, I expect she felt pretty limp when thinking matters calmly over after her ladyship's departure. She knew her lover well enough to guess that he would be as wax in the firm hands of his mother, while she herself would not have a chance of opposing her influence against those seeking to draw him away from her. Once again she read through the few schoolboy letters he had written her, and then looked up at the framed photograph that hung above the mantelpiece of her little bedroom. The face was that of a frank, pleasant-looking young fellow, lightened by eyes somewhat large for a man, but spoiled by a painfully weak mouth. The more Mary Sewell thought, the more sure she felt in her own mind that he loved her, and had meant honestly by her. Did the matter rest with him, she might reckon on being the future Countess of —-, but, unfortunately for her, the person to be considered was not Lord C—-, but the present Countess of —-. From childhood, through boyhood, into manhood it had never once occurred to Lord C—- to dispute a single command of his mother's, and his was not the type of brain to readily receive new ideas. If she was to win in the unequal contest it would have to be by art, not by strength. She sat down and wrote a letter which under all the circumstances was a model of diplomacy. She knew that it would be read by the countess, and, writing it, she kept both mother and son in mind. She made no reproaches, and indulged in but little sentiment. It was the letter of a woman who could claim rights, but who asked only for courtesy. It stated her wish to see him alone and obtain from his own lips the assurance that he wished their engagement to cease. "Do not fear," Mary Sewell wrote, "that I shall be any annoyance to you. My own pride would not let me urge you to marry me against your desire, and I care for you too much to cause you any pain. Assure me with your own lips that you wish our engagement to be at an end, and I shall release you without another word."

The family were in town, and Mary sent her letter by a trusty hand. The countess read it with huge satisfaction, and, re-sealing it, gave it herself into her son's hands. It promised a happy solution of the problem. In imagination, she had all the night been listening to a vulgar breach of promise case. She herself had been submitted to a most annoying cross-examination by a pert barrister. Her son's assumption of the name of Robinson had been misunderstood and severely commented upon by the judge. A sympathetic jury had awarded thumping damages, and for the next six months the family title would be a peg on which music-hall singers and comic journalists would hang their ribald jokes. Lord C—- read the letter, flushed, and dutifully handed it back to his mother. She made pretence to read it as for the first time, and counselled him to accord the interview.

"I am so glad," she said, "that the girl is taking the matter sensibly. We must really do something for her in the future, when everything is settled. Let her ask for me, and then the servants will fancy she's a lady's maid or something of that sort, come after a place, and won't talk."

So that evening Mary Sewell, addressed by the butler as "young woman," was ushered into the small drawing-room that connects the library of No. —- Grosvenor Square with the other reception rooms. The countess, now all amiability, rose to meet her.

"My son will be here in a moment," she explained, "he has informed me of the purport of your letter. Believe me, my dear Miss Sewell, no one can regret his thoughtless conduct more than I do. But young men will be young men, and they do not stop to reflect that what may be a joke to them may be taken quite seriously by others."

"I don't regard the matter as a joke, my lady," replied Mary somewhat curtly.

"Of course not, my dear," added the countess, "that's what I'm saying. It was very wrong of him altogether. But with your pretty face, you will not, I am sure, have long to wait for a husband; we must see what we can do for you."

The countess certainly lacked tact; it must have handicapped her exceedingly.

"Thank you," answered the girl, "but I prefer to choose my own."

Fortunately — or the interview might have ended in another quarrel — the cause of all the trouble at this moment entered the room, and the countess, whispering a few final words of instruction to him as she passed out, left them together.

Mary took a chair in the centre of the room, at equal distance from both doors. Lord C—-, finding any sort of a seat uncomfortable under the circumstances, preferred to stand with his back to the mantelpiece. Dead silence was maintained for a few seconds, and then Mary, drawing the daintiest of handkerchiefs from her pocket, began to cry. The countess must have been a poor diplomatist, or she might have thought of this; or she may have remembered her own appearance on the rare occasions when she herself, a big, raw-boned girl, had attempted the softening influence of tears, and have attached little importance to the possibility. But when these soft, dimpled women cry, and cry quietly, it is another matter. Their eyes grow brighter, and the tears, few and far between, lie like dewdrops on a rose leaf.

Lord C—- was as tender-hearted a lout as ever lived. In a moment he was on his knees with his arm round the girl's waist, pouring out such halting words of love and devotion as came to his unready brain, cursing his fate, his earldom, and his mother, and assuring Mary that his only chance of happiness lay in his making her his countess. Had Mary liked to say the word at that moment, he would have caught her to his arms, and defied the whole world — for the time being. But Mary was a very practical young woman, and there are difficulties in the way of handling a lover, who, however ready he may be to do your bidding so long as your eyes are upon him, is liable to be turned from his purpose so soon as another influence is substituted for your own. His lordship suggested an immediate secret marriage. But you cannot run out into the street, knock up a clergyman, and get married on the spot, and Mary knew that the moment she was gone his lordship's will would revert to his mother's keeping. Then his lordship suggested flight, but flight requires money, and the countess knew enough to keep his lordship's purse in her own hands. Despair seized upon his lordship.

"It's no use," he cried, "it will end in my marrying her."

"Who's she?" exclaimed Mary somewhat quickly.

His lordship explained the position. The family estates were heavily encumbered. It was deemed advisable that his lordship should marry Money, and Money, in the person of the only daughter of rich and ambitious parvenus, had offered itself — or, to speak more correctly, had been offered.

"What's she like?" asked Mary.

"Oh, she's nice enough," was the reply, "only I don't care for her and she doesn't care for me. It won't be much fun for either of us," and his lordship laughed dismally.

"How do you know she doesn't care for you?" asked Mary. A woman may be critical of her lover's shortcomings, but at the very least he is good enough for every other woman.

"Well, she happens to care for somebody else," answered his lordship, "she told me so herself."

That would account for it.

"And is she willing to marry you?" inquired Mary.

His lordship shrugged his shoulders.

"Oh, well, you know, her people want it," he replied.

In spite of her trouble, the girl could not help a laugh. These young swells seemed to have but small wills of their own. Her ladyship, on the other side of the door, grew nervous. It was the only sound she had been able to hear.

"It's deuced awkward," explained his lordship, "when you're — well, when you are anybody, you know. You can't do as you like. Things are expected of you, and there's such a lot to be considered."

Mary rose and clasped her pretty dimpled hands, from which she had drawn her gloves, behind his neck.

"You do love me, Jack?" she said, looking up into his face.

For answer the lad hugged her to him very tightly, and there were tears in his eyes.

"Look here, Mary," he cried, "if I could only get rid of my position, and settle down with you as a country gentleman, I'd do it tomorrow. Damn the title, it's going to be the curse of my life."

Perhaps in that moment Mary also wished that the title were at the bottom of the sea, and that her lover were only the plain Mr. John Robinson she had thought him. These big, stupid men are often very loveable in spite of, or because of their weakness. They appeal to the mother side of a woman's heart, and that is the biggest side in all good women.

Suddenly however, the door opened. The countess appeared, and sentiment flew out. Lord C——, releasing Mary, sprang back, looking like a guilty school-boy.

"I thought I heard Miss Sewell go out," said her ladyship in the icy tones that had never lost their power of making her son's heart freeze within him. "I want to see you when you are free."

"I shan't be long," stammered his lordship. "Mary — Miss Sewell is just going."

Mary waited without moving until the countess had left and closed the door behind her. Then she turned to her lover and spoke in quick, low tones.

"Give me her address — the girl they want you to marry!"

"What are you going to do?" asked his lordship.

"I don't know," answered the girl, "but I'm going to see her."

She scribbled the name down, and then said, looking the boy squarely in the face:

"Tell me frankly, Jack, do you want to marry me, or do you not?"

"You know I do, Mary," he answered, and his eyes spoke stronger than his words. "If I weren't a silly ass, there would be none of this trouble. But I don't know how it is; I say to myself I'll do, a thing, but the mater talks and talks and —"

"I know," interrupted Mary with a smile. "Don't argue with her, fall in with all her views, and pretend to agree with her."

"If you could only think of some plan," said his lordship, catching at the hope of her words, "you are so clever."

"I am going to try," answered Mary, "and if I fail, you must run off with me, even if you have to do it right before your mother's eyes."

What she meant was, "I shall have to run off with you," but she thought it better to put it the other way about.

Mary found her involuntary rival a meek, gentle little lady, as much under the influence of her blustering father as was Lord C—- under that of his mother. What took place at the interview one can only surmise; but certain it is that the two girls, each for her own ends, undertook to aid and abet one another.

Much to the surprised delight of their respective parents, there came about a change in the attitude hitherto assumed towards one another by Miss Clementina Hodskiss and Lord C—-. All objections to his lordship's unwilling attentions were suddenly withdrawn by the lady. Indeed, so swift to come and go are the whims of women, his calls were actually encouraged, especially when, as generally happened, they coincided with the absence from home of Mr. and Mrs. Hodskiss. Quite as remarkable was the new-born desire of Lord C—- towards Miss Clementina Hodskiss. Mary's name was never mentioned, and the suggestion of immediate marriage was listened to without remonstrance. Wiser folk would have puzzled their brains, but both her ladyship and ex-Contractor Hodskiss were accustomed to find all things yield to their wishes. The countess saw visions of a rehabilitated estate, and Clementina's father dreamed of a peerage, secured by the influence of aristocratic connections. All that the young folks stipulated for (and on that point their firmness was supernatural) was that the marriage should be quiet, almost to the verge of secrecy.

"No beastly fuss," his lordship demanded. "Let it be somewhere in the country, and no mob!" and his mother, thinking she understood his reason, patted his cheek affectionately.

"I should like to go down to Aunt Jane's and be married quietly from there," explained Miss Hodskiss to her father.

Aunt Jane resided on the outskirts of a small Hampshire village, and "sat under" a clergyman famous throughout the neighbourhood for having lost the roof to his mouth.

"You can't be married by that old fool," thundered her father — Mr. Hodskiss always thundered; he thundered even his prayers.

"He christened me," urged Miss Clementina.

"And Lord knows what he called you. Nobody can understand a word he says."

"I'd like him to marry me," reiterated Miss Clementina.

Neither her ladyship nor the contractor liked the idea. The latter in particular had looked forward to a big function, chronicled at length in all the newspapers. But after all, the marriage was the essential thing, and perhaps, having regard to some foolish love passages that had happened between Clementina and a certain penniless naval lieutenant, ostentation might be out of place.

So in due course Clementina departed for Aunt Jane's, accompanied only by her maid.

Quite a treasure was Miss Hodskiss's new maid.

"A clean, wholesome girl," said of her Contractor Hodskiss, who cultivated affability towards the lower orders; "knows her place, and talks sense. You keep that girl, Clemmy."

"Do you think she knows enough?" hazarded the maternal Hodskiss.

"Quite sufficient for any decent woman," retorted the contractor. "When Clemmy wants painting and stuffing, it will be time enough for her to think about getting one of your '*Ach Himmels*' or '*Mon Dieus*'."

"I like the girl myself immensely," agreed Clementina's mother. "You can trust her, and she doesn't give herself airs."

Her praises reached even the countess, suffering severely at the moment from the tyranny of an elderly Fraulein.

"I must see this treasure," thought the countess to herself. "I am tired of these foreign minxes."

But no matter at what cunning hour her ladyship might call, the "treasure" always happened for some reason or other to be abroad.

"Your girl is always out when I come," laughed the countess. "One would fancy there was some reason for it."

"It does seem odd," agreed Clementina, with a slight flush.

Miss Hodskiss herself showed rather than spoke her appreciation of the girl. She seemed unable to move or think without her. Not even from the interviews with Lord C—- was the maid always absent.

The marriage, it was settled, should be by licence. Mrs. Hodskiss made up her mind at first to run down and see to the preliminaries, but really when the time arrived it hardly seemed necessary to take that trouble. The ordering of the whole affair was so very simple, and the "treasure" appeared to understand the business most thoroughly, and to be willing to take the whole burden upon her own shoulders. It was not, therefore, until the evening before the wedding that the Hodskiss family arrived in force, filling Aunt Jane's small dwelling to its utmost capacity. The swelling figure of the contractor, standing beside the tiny porch, compelled the passer-by to think of the doll's house in which the dwarf resides during fair-time, ringing his own bell out of his own first-floor window. The countess and Lord C—- were staying with her ladyship's sister, the Hon. Mrs. J—-, at G—- Hall, some ten miles distant, and were to drive over in the morning. The then Earl of —-

was in Norway, salmon fishing. Domestic events did not interest him.

Clementina complained of a headache after dinner, and went to bed early. The "treasure" also was indisposed. She seemed worried and excited.

"That girl is as eager about the thing," remarked Mrs. Hodskiss, "as though it was her own marriage."

In the morning Clementina was still suffering from her headache, but asserted her ability to go through the ceremony, provided everybody would keep away, and not worry her. The "treasure" was the only person she felt she could bear to have about her. Half an hour before it was time to start for church her mother looked her up again. She had grown still paler, if possible, during the interval, and also more nervous and irritable. She threatened to go to bed and stop there if she was not left quite alone. She almost turned her mother out of the room, locking the door behind her. Mrs. Hodskiss had never known her daughter to be like this before.

The others went on, leaving her to follow in the last carriage with her father. The contractor, forewarned, spoke little to her. Only once he had occasion to ask her a question, and then she answered in a strained, unnatural voice. She appeared, so far as could be seen under her heavy veil, to be crying.

"Well, this is going to be a damned cheerful wedding," said Mr. Hodskiss, and lapsed into sulkiness.

The wedding was not so quiet as had been anticipated. The village had got scent of it, and had spread itself upon the event, while half the house party from G—- Hall had insisted on driving over to take part in the proceedings. The little church was better filled than it had been for many a long year past.

The presence of the stylish crowd unnerved the ancient clergyman, long unaccustomed to the sight of a strange face, and the first sound of the ancient clergyman's voice unnerved the stylish crowd. What little articulation he possessed entirely disappeared, no one could understand a word he said. He appeared to be uttering sounds of distress. The ancient gentleman's infliction had to be explained in low asides, and it also had to be explained why such an one had been chosen to perform the ceremony.

"It was a whim of Clementina's," whispered her mother. "Her father and myself were married from here, and he christened her. The dear child's full of sentiment. I think it so nice of her."

Everybody agreed it was charming, but wished it were over. The general effect was weird in the extreme.

Lord C—- spoke up fairly well, but the bride's responses were singularly indistinct, the usual order of things being thus reversed. The story of the naval lieutenant was remembered, and added to, and some of the more sentimental of the women began to cry in sympathy.

In the vestry things assumed a brighter tone. There was no lack of witnesses to sign the register. The verger pointed out to them the place, and they wrote their names, as people in such cases do, without stopping to read. Then it occurred to some one that the bride had not yet signed. She stood apart, with her veil still down, and appeared to have been forgotten. Encouraged, she came forward meekly, and took the pen from the hand of the verger. The countess came and stood behind her.

"Mary," wrote the bride, in a hand that looked as though it ought to have been firm, but which was not.

"Dear me," said the countess, "I never knew there was a Mary in your name. How differently you write when you write slowly."

The bride did not answer, but followed with "Susannah."

"Why, what a lot of names you must have, my dear!" exclaimed the countess. "When are you going to get to the ones we all know?"

"Ruth," continued the bride without answering.

Breeding is not always proof against strong emotion. The countess snatched the bride's veil from her face, and Mary Susannah Ruth Sewell stood before her, flushed and trembling, but looking none the less pretty because of that. At this point the crowd came in useful.

"I am sure your ladyship does not wish a scene," said Mary, speaking low. "The thing is done."

"The thing can be undone, and will be," retorted the countess in the same tone. "You, you —"

"My wife, don't forget that, mother," said Lord C—- coming between them, and slipping Mary's hand on to his arm. "We are both sorry to have had to go about the thing in this roundabout way, but we wanted to avoid a fuss. I think we had better be getting away. I'm afraid Mr. Hodskiss is going to be noisy."

The doctor poured himself out a glass of claret, and drank it off. His throat must have been dry.

"And what became of Clementina?" I asked. "Did the naval lieutenant, while the others were at church, dash up in a post-chaise and carry her off?"

"That's what ought to have happened, for the whole thing to be in keeping," agreed the doctor. "I believe as a matter of fact she did marry him eventually, but not till some years later, after the contractor had died."

"And did Mr. Hodskiss make a noise in the vestry?" I persisted. The doctor never will finish a story.

"I can't say for certain," answered my host, "I only saw the gentleman once. That was at a shareholders' meeting. I should incline to the opinion that he did."

"I suppose the bride and bridegroom slipped out as quietly as possible and drove straight off," I suggested.

"That would have been the sensible thing for them to do," agreed the doctor.

"But how did she manage about her travelling frock?" I continued. "She could hardly have gone back to her Aunt Jane's and changed her things." The doctor has no mind for minutiæ.

"I cannot tell you about all that," he replied. "I think I mentioned that Mary was a practical girl. Possibly she had thought of these details."

"And did the countess take the matter quietly?" I asked.

I like a tidy story, where everybody is put into his or her proper place at the end. Your modern romance leaves half his characters lying about just anyhow.

"That also I cannot tell you for certain," answered the doctor, "but I give her credit for so much sense. Lord C—- was of age, and with Mary at his elbow, quite knew his own mind. I believe they travelled for two or three years. The first time I myself set eyes on the countess (*née* Mary Sewell) was just after the late earl's death. I thought she looked a countess, every inch of her, but then I had not heard the story. I mistook the dowager for the housekeeper."

BLASÉ BILLY

It was towards the end of August. He and I appeared to be the only two men left to the Club. He was sitting by an open window, the *Times* lying on the floor beside him. I drew my chair a little closer and remarked: — "Good morning."

He suppressed a yawn, and replied "Mornin'" — dropping the "g." The custom was just coming into fashion; he was always correct.

"Going to be a very hot day, I am afraid," I continued.

"'Fraid so," was the response, after which he turned his head away and gently closed his eyes.

I opined that conversation was not to his wish, but this only made me more determined to talk, and to talk to him above all others in London. The desire took hold of me to irritate him — to break down the imperturbable calm within which he moved and had his being; and I gathered myself together, and settled down to the task.

"Interesting paper the *Times*," I observed.

"Very," he replied, taking it from the floor and handing it to me. "Won't you read it?"

I had been careful to throw into my voice an aggressive cheeriness which I had calculated would vex him, but his manner remained that of a man who is simply bored. I argued with him politely concerning the paper; but he insisted, still with the same weary air, that he had done with it. I thanked him effusively. I judged that he hated effusiveness.

"They say that to read a *Times* leader," I persisted, "is a lesson in English composition."

"So I've been told," he answered tranquilly. "Personally I don't take them."

The *Times*, I could see, was not going to be of much assistance to me. I lit a cigarette, and remarked that he was not shooting. He admitted the fact. Under the circumstances, it would have taxed him to deny it, but the necessity for confession aroused him.

"To myself," he said, "a tramp through miles of mud, in company with four gloomy men in black velveteen, a couple of depressed-looking dogs, and a heavy gun, the entire cavalcade being organised for the purpose of killing some twelve-and-sixpence worth of poultry, suggests the disproportionate."

I laughed boisterously, and cried, "Good, good — very good!"

He was the type of man that shudders inwardly at the sound of laughter. I had the will to slap him on the back, but I thought maybe that would send him away altogether.

I asked him if he hunted. He replied that fourteen hours' talk a day about horses, and only about horses tired him, and that in consequence he had abandoned hunting.

"You fish?" I said.

"I was never sufficiently imaginative," he answered.

"You travel a good deal," I suggested.

He had apparently made up his mind to abandon himself to his fate, for he turned towards me with a resigned air. An ancient nurse of mine had always described me as the most "wearing" child she had ever come across. I prefer to speak of myself as persevering.

"I should go about more," he said, "were I able to see any difference between one place and another."

"Tried Central Africa?" I inquired.

"Once or twice," he answered. "It always reminds me of Kew Gardens."

"China?" I hazarded.

"Cross between a willow-pattern plate and a New York slum," was his comment.

"The North Pole?" I tried, thinking the third time might be lucky.

"Never got quite up to it," he returned. "Reached Cape Hakluyt once."

"How did that impress you?" I asked.

"It didn't impress me," he replied.

The talk drifted to women and bogus companies, dogs, literature, and such-like matters. I found him well informed upon and bored by all.

"They used to be amusing," he said, speaking of the first named, "until they began to take themselves seriously. Now they are merely silly."

I was forced into closer companionship with "Blasé Billy" that autumn, for by chance a month later he and I found ourselves the guests of the same delightful hostess, and I came to liking him better. He was a useful man to have about one. In matters of fashion one could always feel safe following his lead. One knew that his necktie, his collar, his socks, if not the very newest departure, were always correct; and upon social paths, as guide, philosopher, and friend, he was invaluable. He knew every one, together with his or her previous convictions. He was acquainted with every woman's past, and shrewdly surmised every man's future. He could point you out the coal-shed where the Countess of Glenleman had gambolled in her days of innocence, and would take you to breakfast at the coffee-shop off the Mile End Road where "Sam. Smith, Estd. 1820," own brother to the world-famed society novelist, Smith-Stratford, lived an uncriticised, unparagraphed, unphotographed existence upon the profits of "rashers" at three-ha'pence and "door-steps" at two a penny. He knew at what houses it was inadvisable to introduce soap, and at what tables it would be bad form to denounce political jobbery. He could tell you offhand what trademark went with what crest, and remembered the price paid for every baronetcy created during the last twenty-five years.

Regarding himself, he might have made claim with King Charles never to have said a foolish thing, and never to have done a wise one. He despised, or affected to despise, most of his fellow-men, and those of his fellow-men whose opinion was most worth having unaffectedly despised him.

Shortly described, one might have likened him to a Gaiety Johnny with brains. He was capital company after dinner, but in the early morning one avoided him.

So I thought of him until one day he fell in love; or to put it in the words of Teddy Tidmarsh, who brought the news to us, "got mashed on Gerty Lovell."

"The red-haired one," Teddy explained, to distinguish her from her sister, who had lately adopted the newer golden shade.

"Gerty Lovell!" exclaimed the captain, "why, I've always been told the Lovell girls hadn't a penny among them."

"The old man's stone broke, I know for a certainty," volunteered Teddy, who picked up a mysterious but, in other respects, satisfactory income in an office near Hatton Garden, and who was candour itself concerning the private affairs of everybody but himself.

"Oh, some rich pork-packing or diamond-sweating uncle has cropped up in Australia, or America, or one of those places," suggested the captain, "and Billy's got wind of it in good time. Billy knows his way about."

We agreed that some such explanation was needed, though in all other respects Gerty Lovell was just the girl that Reason (not always consulted on these occasions) might herself have chosen for "Blasé Billy's" mate.

The sunlight was not too kind to her, but at evening parties, where the lighting has been well considered, I have seen her look quite girlish. At her best she was not beautiful, but at her worst there was about her an air of breeding and distinction that always saved her from being passed over, and she dressed to perfection. In character she was the typical society woman: always charming, generally insincere. She went to Kensington for her religion and to Mayfair for her morals; accepted her literature from Mudie's and her art from the Grosvenor Gallery; and could and would gabble philanthropy, philosophy, and politics with equal fluency at every five-o'clock tea-table she visited. Her ideas could always be guaranteed as the very latest, and her opinion as that of the person to whom she was talking. Asked by a famous novelist one afternoon, at the Pioneer Club, to give him some idea of her, little Mrs. Bund, the painter's wife, had remained for a few moments with her pretty lips pursed, and had then said:

"She is a woman to whom life could bring nothing more fully satisfying than a dinner invitation from a duchess, and whose nature would be incapable of sustaining deeper suffering than that caused by an ill-fitting costume."

At the time I should have said the epigram was as true as it was cruel, but I suppose we none of us quite know each other.

I congratulated "Blasé Billy," or to drop his Club nickname and give him the full benefit of his social label, "The Hon. William Cecil Wychwood Stanley Drayton," on the occasion of our next meeting, which happened upon the steps of the Savoy Restaurant, and I thought — unless a quiver of the electric light deceived me — that he blushed.

"Charming girl," I said. "You're a lucky dog, Billy."

It was the phrase that custom demands upon such occasions, and it came of its own accord to my tongue without costing me the trouble of composition, but he seized upon it as though it had been a gem of friendly sincerity.

"You will like her even more when you know her better," he said. "She is so different from the usual woman that one meets. Come and see her to-morrow afternoon, she will be so pleased. Go about four, I will tell her to expect you."

I rang the bell at ten minutes past five. Billy was there. She greeted me with a little tremor of embarrassment, which sat oddly upon her, but which was not altogether unpleasing. She said it was kind of me to come so early. I stayed for about half an hour, but conversation flagged, and some of my cleverest remarks attracted no attention whatever.

When I rose to take my leave, Billy said that he must be off too, and that he would accompany me. Had they been ordinary lovers, I should have been careful to give them an opportunity of making their adieus in secret; but in the case of the Honourable William Drayton and the eldest Miss Lovell I concluded that such tactics were needless, so I waited till he had shaken hands, and went downstairs with him.

But in the hall Billy suddenly ejaculated, "By Jove! Half a minute," and ran back up the stairs three at a time. Apparently he found what he had gone for on the landing, for I did not hear the opening of the drawing-room door. Then the Honourable Billy redescended with a sober, nonchalant air.

"Left my gloves behind me," he explained, as he took my arm. "I am always leaving my gloves about."

I did not mention that I had seen him take them from his hat and slip them into his coat-tail pocket.

We at the Club did not see very much of Billy during the next three months, but the captain, who prided himself upon his playing of the *rôle* of smoking-room cynic — though he would have been better in the part had he occasionally displayed a little originality — was of opinion that our loss would be more than made up to us after the marriage. Once in the twilight I caught sight of a figure that reminded me of Billy's, accompanied by a figure that might have been that of the eldest Miss Lovell; but as the spot was Battersea Park, which is not a fashionable evening promenade, and the two figures were holding each other's hands, the whole picture being suggestive of the closing chapter of a *London Journal* romance, I concluded I had made an error.

But I did see them in the Adelphi stalls one evening, rapt in a sentimental melodrama. I joined them between the acts, and poked fun at the play, as one does at the Adelphi, but Miss Lovell begged me quite earnestly not to spoil her interest, and Billy wanted to enter upon a serious argument as to whether a man was justified in behaving as Will Terriss had just behaved towards the woman he loved. I left them and returned to my own party, to the satisfaction, I am inclined to think, of all concerned.

They married in due course. We were mistaken on one point. She brought Billy nothing. But they both seemed quite content on his not too extravagant fortune. They took a tiny house not far from Victoria Station, and hired a brougham for the season. They did not entertain very much, but they contrived to be seen everywhere it was right and fashionable they should be seen. The Honourable Mrs. Drayton was a much younger and brighter person than had been the eldest Miss Lovell, and as she continued to dress charmingly, her social position rose rapidly. Billy went everywhere with her, and evidently took a keen pride in her success. It was even said that he designed her dresses for her, and I have myself seen him earnestly studying the costumes in Russell and Allen's windows.

The captain's prophecy remained unfulfilled. "Blasé Billy" — if the name could still be applied to him — hardly ever visited the Club after his marriage. But I had grown to like him, and, as he had foretold, to like his wife. I found their calm indifference to the burning questions of the day a positive relief from the strenuous atmosphere of literary and artistic circles. In the drawing-room of their little house in Eaton Row, the comparative merits of George Meredith and George R. Sims were not considered worth discussion. Both were regarded as persons who afforded a certain amount of amusement in return for a certain amount of cash. And on any Wednesday afternoon, Henrick Ibsen and Arthur Roberts would have been equally welcome, as adding piquancy to the small gathering. Had I been compelled to pass my life in such a house, this Philistine attitude might have palled upon me; but, under the circumstances, it refreshed me, and I made use of my welcome, which I believe was genuine, to its full extent.

As months went by, they seemed to me to draw closer to one another, though I am given to understand that such is not the rule in fashionable circles. One evening I arrived a little before my time, and was shown up into the drawing-room by the soft-footed butler. They were sitting in the dusk with their arms round one another. It was impossible to withdraw, so I faced the situation and coughed. A pair of middle-class lovers could not have appeared more awkward or surprised.

But the incident established an understanding between us, and I came to be regarded as a friend before whom there was less necessity to act.

Studying them, I came to the conclusion that the ways and manners of love are very same-like throughout the world, as though the foolish boy, unheedful of human advance, kept but one school for minor poet and East End shop-boy, for Girton girl and little milliner; taught but the one lesson to the end-of-the-nineteenth-century Johnny that he taught to bearded Pict and Hun four thousand years ago.

Thus the summer and the winter passed pleasantly for the Honourable Billy, and then, as luck would have it, he fell ill just in the very middle of the London season, when invitations to balls and dinner parties, luncheons and "At Homes," were pouring in from every quarter; when the lawns at Hurlingham were at their smoothest, and the paddocks at their smartest.

It was unfortunate, too, that the fashions that season suited the Honourable Mrs. Billy as they had not suited her for years. In the early spring, she and Billy had been hard at work planning costumes calculated to cause a flutter through Mayfair, and the dresses and the bonnets — each one a work of art — were waiting on their stands to do their killing work. But the Honourable Mrs. Billy, for the first time in her life, had lost interest in such things.

Their friends were genuinely sorry, for society was Billy's element, and in it he was interesting and amusing. But, as Lady Gower said, there was no earthly need for his wife to constitute herself a prisoner. Her shutting herself off from the world could do him no good and it would look odd.

Accordingly the Honourable Mrs. Drayton, to whom oddness was a crime, and the voice of Lady Gower as the voice of duty, sacrificed her inclinations on the social shrine, laced the new costumes tight across her aching heart, and went down into society.

But the Honourable Mrs. Drayton achieved not the success of former seasons. Her small talk grew so very small, that even Park Lane found it unsatisfying. Her famous laugh rang mechanically. She smiled at the wisdom of dukes, and became sad at the funny stories of millionaires. Society voted her a good wife but bad company, and confined its attentions to cards of inquiry. And for this relief the Honourable Mrs. Drayton was grateful, for Billy waned weaker and weaker. In the world of shadows in which she moved, he was the one real thing. She was of very little practical use, but it comforted her to think that she was helping to nurse him.

But Billy himself it troubled.

"I do wish you would go out more," he would say. "It makes me feel that I'm such a selfish brute, keeping you tied up here in this dismal little house. Besides," he would add, "people miss you; they will hate me for keeping you away." For, where his wife was concerned, Billy's knowledge of the world availed him little. He really thought society craved for the Honourable Mrs. Drayton, and would not be comforted where she was not.

"I would rather stop with you, dear," would be the answer; "I don't care to go about by myself. You must get well quickly and take me."

And so the argument continued, until one evening, as she sat by herself, the nurse entered softly, closed the door behind her, and came over to her.

"I wish you would go out to-night, ma'am," said the nurse, "just for an hour or two. I think it would please the master; he is worrying himself because he thinks it is his fault that you do not; and just now" — the woman hesitated for a moment — "just now I want to keep him very quiet."

"Is he weaker, nurse?"

"Well, he is not stronger, ma'am, and I think — I think we must humour him."

The Honourable Mrs. Drayton rose, and, crossing to the window, stood for a while looking out.

"But where am I to go, nurse?" she said at length, turning with a smile. "I've no invitations anywhere."

"Can't you make believe to have one?" said the nurse. "It is only seven o'clock. Say you are going to a dinner-party; you can come home early then. Go and dress yourself, and come down and say good-bye to him, and then come in again about eleven, as though you had just returned."

"You think I must, nurse?"

"I think it would be better, ma'am. I wish you would try it."

The Honourable Mrs. Drayton went to the door, then paused.

"He has such sharp ears, nurse; he will listen for the opening of the door and the sound of the carriage."

"I will see to that," said the nurse. "I will tell them to have the carriage here at ten minutes to eight. Then you can drive to the end of the street, slip out, and walk back. I will let you in myself."

"And about coming home?" asked the other woman.

"You must slip out for a few minutes before eleven, and the carriage must be waiting for you at the corner again. Leave all that to me."

In half an hour the Honourable Mrs. Drayton entered the sick-room, radiant in evening dress and jewels. Fortunately the lights were low, or "Blasé-Billy" might have been doubtful as to the effect his wife was likely to produce. For her face was not the face that one takes to dinner-parties.

"Nurse tells me you are going to the Grevilles this evening. I am so glad. I've been worrying myself about you, moped up here right through the season."

He took her hands in his and held her out at arm's length from him.

"How handsome you look, dear!" he said. "How they must have all been cursing me for keeping you shut up here, like a princess in an ogre's castle! I shall never dare to face them again."

She laughed, well pleased at his words.

"I shall not be late," she said. "I shall be so anxious to get back and see how my boy has behaved. If you have not been good I shan't go again."

They kissed and parted, and at eleven she returned to the room. She told him what a delightful evening it had been, and bragged a little of her own success.

The nurse told her that he had been more cheerful that evening than for many nights.

So every day the farce was played for him. One day it was to a luncheon that she went, in a costume by Redfern; the next night to a ball, in a frock direct from Paris; again to an "At Home," or concert, or dinner-party. Loafers and passers-by would stop to stare at a haggard, red-eyed woman, dressed as for a drawing-room, slipping thief-like in and out of her own door.

I heard them talking of her one afternoon, at a house where I called, and I joined the group to listen.

"I always thought her heartless, but I gave her credit for sense," a woman was saying. "One doesn't expect a woman to be fond of her husband, but she needn't make a parade of ignoring him when he is dying."

I pleaded absence from town to inquire what was meant, and from all lips I heard the same account. One had noticed her carriage at the door two or three evenings in succession. Another had seen her returning home. A third had seen her coming out, and so on.

I could not fit the fact in with my knowledge of her, so the next evening I called. The door was opened instantly by herself.

"I saw you from the window," she said. "Come in here; don't speak."

I followed her, and she closed the door behind her. She was dressed in a magnificent costume, her hair sparkling with diamonds, and I looked my questions.

She laughed bitterly.

"I am supposed to be at the opera to-night," she explained. "Sit down, if you have a few minutes to spare."

I said it was for a talk that I had come; and there, in the dark room, lighted only by the street lamp without, she told me all. And at the end she dropped her head on her bare arms; and I turned away and looked out of the window for a while.

"I feel so ridiculous," she said, rising and coming towards me. "I sit here all the evening dressed like this. I'm afraid I don't act my part very well; but, fortunately, dear Billy never was much of a judge of art, and it is good enough for him. I tell him the most awful lies about what everybody has said to me, and what I've said to everybody, and how my gowns were admired. What do you think of this one?"

For answer I took the privilege of a friend.

"I'm glad you think well of me," she said. "Billy has such a high opinion of you. You will hear some funny tales. I'm glad you know."

I had to leave London again, and Billy died before I returned. I heard that she had to be fetched from a ball, and was only just in time to touch his lips before they were cold. But her friends excused her by saying that the end had come very suddenly.

I called on her a little later, and before I left I hinted to her what people were saying, and asked her if I had not better tell them the truth.

"I would rather you didn't," she answered. "It seems like making public the secret side of one's life."

"But," I urged, "they will think —"

She interrupted me.

"Does it matter very much what they think?"

Which struck me as a very remarkable sentiment, coming from the Hon. Mrs. Drayton, *née* the elder Miss Lovell.

THE CHOICE OF CYRIL HARJOHN

Between a junior resident master of twenty-one, and a backward lad of fifteen, there yawns an impassable gulf. Between a struggling journalist of one-and-thirty, and an M.D. of twenty-five, with a brilliant record behind him, and a career of exceptional promise before him, a close friendship is however permissible.

My introduction to Cyril Harjohn was through the Rev. Charles Fauerberg.

"Our young friend," said the Rev. Mr. Fauerberg, standing in the most approved tutorial attitude, with his hand upon his pupil's shoulder, "our young friend has been somewhat neglected, but I see in him possibilities warranting hope — warranting, I may say, very great hope. For the present he will be under my especial care, and you will not therefore concern yourself with his studies. He will sleep with Milling and the others in dormitory number two."

The lad formed a liking for me, and I think, and hope, I rendered his sojourn at "Alpha House" less irksome than otherwise it might have been. The Reverend Charles' method with the backward was on all fours with that adopted for the bringing on of geese; he cooped them up and crammed them. The process is profitable to the trainer, but painful to the goose.

Young Harjohn and myself left "Alpha House" at the end of the same term; he bound for Brasenose, I for Bloomsbury. He made a point of never coming up to London without calling on me, when we would dine together in one of Soho's many dingy, garlic-scented restaurants, and afterwards, over our bottle of cheap Beaune, discuss the coming of our lives; and when he entered Guy's I left John Street, and took chambers close to his in Staple Inn. Those were pleasant days. Childhood is an over-rated period, fuller of sorrow than of joy. I would not take my childhood back, were it a gift, but I would give the rest of my life to live the twenties over again.

To Cyril I was the man of the world, and he looked to me for wisdom, not seeing always, I fear, that he got it; while from him I gathered enthusiasm, and learnt the profit that comes to a man from the keeping of ideals.

Often as we have talked, I have felt as though a visible light came from him, framing his face as with the halo of some pictured saint. Nature had wasted him, putting him into this nineteenth century of ours. Her victories are accomplished. Her army of heroes, the few sung, the many forgotten, is disbanded. The long peace won by their blood and pain is settled on the land. She had fashioned Cyril Harjohn for one of her soldiers. He would have been a martyr, in the days when thought led to the stake, a fighter for the truth, when to speak one's mind meant death. To lead some forlorn hope for Civilisation would have been his true work; Fate had condemned him to sentry duty in a well-ordered barrack.

But there is work to be done in the world, though the labour lies now in the vineyard, not on the battlefield. A small but sufficient fortune purchased for him freedom. To most men an assured income is the grave of ambition; to Cyril it was the foundation of desire. Relieved from the necessity of working to live, he could afford the luxury of living to work. His profession was to him a passion; he regarded it, not with the cold curiosity of the scholar, but with the imaginative devotion of the disciple. To help to push its frontiers forward, to carry its flag farther into the untravelled desert that ever lies beyond the moving boundary of human knowledge, was his dream.

One summer evening, I remember, we were sitting in his rooms, and during a silence there came to us through the open window the moaning of the city, as of a tired child. He rose and stretched his arms out towards the darkening streets, as if he would gather to him all the toiling men and women and comfort them.

"Oh, that I could help you!" he cried, "my brothers and my sisters. Take my life, oh God, and spend it for me among your people."

The speech sounds theatrical, as I read it, written down, but to the young such words are not ridiculous, as to us older men.

In the natural order of events, he fell in love, and with just the woman one would expect him to be attracted by. Elspeth Grant was of the type from which the world, by instinct rather than by convention, has drawn its Madonnas and its saints. To describe a woman in words is impossible. Her beauty was not a possession to be catalogued, but herself. One felt it as one feels the beauty of a summer's dawn breaking the shadows of a sleeping city, but one cannot set it down. I often met her, and, when talking to her, I knew myself — I, hack-journalist, frequenter of Fleet Street bars, retailer of smoke-room stories — a great gentleman, incapable of meanness, fit for all noble deeds.

In her presence life became a thing beautiful and gracious; a school for courtesy, and tenderness, and simplicity.

I have wondered since, coming to see a little more clearly into the ways of men, whether it would not have been better had she been less spiritual, had her nature possessed a greater alloy of earth, making it more fit for the uses of this work-a-day world. But at the time, these two friends of mine seemed to me to have been created for one another.

She appealed to all that was highest in Cyril's character, and he worshipped her with an unconcealed adoration that, from any man less high-minded, would have appeared affectation, and which she accepted with the sweet content that Artemis might have accorded to the homage of Endymion.

There was no formal engagement between them. Cyril seemed to shrink from the materialising of his love by any thought of marriage. To him she was an ideal of womanhood rather than a flesh-and-blood woman. His love for her was a religion; it had no taint of earthly passion in its composition.

Had I known the world better I might have anticipated the result; for the red blood ran in my friend's veins; and, alas, we dream our poems, not live them. But at the time, the idea of any other woman coming between them would have appeared to me folly. The suggestion that that other woman might be Geraldine Fawley I should have resented as an insult to my intelligence: that is the point of the story I do not understand to this day.

That he should be attracted by her, that he should love to linger near her, watching the dark flush come and go across her face, seeking to call the fire into her dark eyes was another matter, and quite comprehensible; for the girl was wonderfully handsome, with a bold, voluptuous beauty which invited while it dared. But considered in any other light than that of an animal, she repelled. At times when, for her ends, it seemed worth the exertion, she would assume a certain wayward sweetness, but her acting was always clumsy and exaggerated, capable of deceiving no one but a fool.

Cyril, at all events, was not taken in by it. One evening, at a Bohemian gathering, the *entrée* to which was notoriety rather than character, they had been talking together for some considerable time when, wishing to speak to Cyril, I strolled up to join them. As I came towards them she moved away, her dislike for me being equal to mine for her; a thing which was, perhaps, well for me.

"Miss Fawley prefers two as company to three," I observed, looking after her retreating figure.

"I am afraid she finds you what we should call an anti-sympathetic element," he replied, laughing.

"Do you like her?" I asked him, somewhat bluntly.

His eyes rested upon her as she stood in the doorway, talking to a small, black-bearded man who had just been introduced to her. After a few moments she went out upon his arm, and then Cyril turned to me.

"I think her," he replied, speaking, as was necessary, very low, "the embodiment of all that is evil in womanhood. In old days she would have been a Cleopatra, a Theodora, a Delilah. To-day, lacking opportunity, she is the 'smart woman' grubbing for an opening into society — and old Fawley's daughter. I'm tired; let us go home."

His allusion to her parentage was significant. Few people thought of connecting clever, handsome Geraldine Fawley with "Rogue Fawley," Jew renegade, ex-gaol bird, and outside broker; who, having expectations from his daughter, took care not to hamper her by ever being seen in her company. But no one who had once met the father could ever forget the relationship while talking to the daughter. The older face, with its cruelty, its cunning, and its greed stood reproduced, feature for feature, line for line. It was as though Nature, for an artistic freak, had set herself the task of fashioning hideousness and beauty from precisely the same materials. Between the leer of the man and the smile of the girl, where lay the difference? It would have puzzled any student of anatomy to point it out. Yet the one sickened, while to gain the other most men would have given much.

Cyril's answer to my question satisfied me for the time. He met the girl often, as was natural. She was a singer of some repute, and our social circle was what is commonly called "literary and artistic." To do her justice, however, she made no attempt to fascinate him, nor even to be particularly agreeable to him. Indeed, she seemed to be at pains to show him her natural — in other words, her most objectionable side.

Coming out of the theatre one first night, we met her in the lobby. I was following Cyril at some little distance, but as he stopped to speak to her the movement of the crowd placed me just behind them.

"Will you be at Leightons' to-morrow?" I heard him ask her in a low tone.

"Yes," she answered, "and I wish you wouldn't come."

"Why not?"

"Because you're a fool, and you bore me."

Under ordinary circumstances I should have taken the speech for badinage — it was the kind of wit the woman would have indulged in. But Cyril's face clouded with anger and vexation. I said nothing. I did not wish him to know that I had overheard. I tried to believe that he was amusing himself, but my own explanation did not satisfy me.

Next evening I went to Leightons' by myself. The Grants were in town, and Cyril was dining with them. I found I did not know many people, and cared little for those I did. I was about to escape when Miss Fawley's name was announced. I was close to the door, and she had to stop and speak to me. We exchanged a few common-places. She either made love to a man or was rude to him. She gener-ally talked to me without looking at me, nodding and smiling meanwhile to people around. I have met many women equally ill-mannered, and without her excuse. For a moment, however, she turned her eyes to mine.

"Where's your friend, Mr. Harjohn?" she asked. "I thought you were inseparables."

I looked at her in astonishment.

"He is dining out to-night," I replied. "I do not think he will come."

She laughed. I think it was the worst part about the woman, her laugh; it suggested so much cruelty.

"I think he will," she said.

It angered me into an indiscretion. She was moving away. I stepped in front of her and stopped her.

"What makes you think so?" I asked, and my voice, I know, betrayed the anxiety I felt as to her reply. She looked me straight in the face. There was one virtue she possessed — the virtue that ani-mals hold above mankind — truthfulness. She knew I disliked her — hate would be, perhaps, a more exact expression, did not the word sound out of date, and she made no pretence of not knowing it and returning the compliment.

"Because I am here," she answered. "Why don't you save him? Have you no influence over him? Tell the Saint to keep him; I don't want him. You heard what I said to him last night. I shall only marry him for the sake of his position, and the money he can earn if he likes to work and not play the fool. Tell him what I have said; I shan't deny it."

She passed on to greet a decrepit old lord with a languishing smile, and I stood staring after her with, I fear, a somewhat stupid expression, until some young fool came up grinning, to ask me whether I had seen a ghost or backed a "wrong 'un."

There was no need to wait; I felt no curiosity. Something told me the woman had spoken the truth. It was mere want of motive that made me linger. I saw him come in, and watched him hanging round her, like a dog, waiting for a kind word, or failing that, a look. I knew she saw me, and I knew it added to her zest that I was there. Not till we were in the street did I speak to him. He started as I touched him. We were neither of us good actors. He must have read much in my face, and I saw that he had read it; and we walked side by side in silence, I thinking what to say, wondering whether I should do good or harm, wishing that we were anywhere but in these silent, life-packed streets, so filled with the unseen. It was not until we had nearly reached the Albert Hall that we broke the silence. Then it was he who spoke:

"Do you think I haven't told myself all that?" he said. "Do you think I don't know I'm a damned fool, a cad, a liar! What the devil's the good of talking about it?"

"But I can't understand it," I said.

"No," he replied, "because you're a fool, because you have only seen one side of me. You think me a grand gentleman, because I talk big, and am full of noble sentiment. Why, you idiot, the Devil himself could take you in. *He* has his fine moods, I suppose, talks like a saint, and says his prayers with the rest of us. Do you remember the first night at old Fauerberg's? You poked your silly head into the dormitory, and saw me kneeling by the bedside, while the other fellows stood by grinning. You closed the door softly — you thought I never saw you. I was not praying, I was trying to pray."

"It showed that you had pluck, if it showed nothing else," I answered. "Most boys would not have tried, and you kept it up."

"Ah, yes," he answered, "I promised the Mater I would, and I did. Poor old soul, she was as big a fool as you are. She believed in me. Don't you remember, finding me one Saturday afternoon all alone, stuffing myself with cake and jam?"

I laughed at the recollection, though Heaven knows I was in no laughing mood. I had found him with an array of pastry spread out before him, sufficient to make him ill for a week, and I had boxed his ears, and had thrown the whole collection into the road.

"The Mater gave me half-a-crown a week for pocket-money," he continued, "and I told the fellows I had only a shilling, so that I could gorge myself with the other eighteenpence undisturbed. Pah! I was a little beast even in those days!"

"It was only a schoolboy trick," I argued, "it was natural enough."

"Yes," he answered, "and this is only a man's trick, and is natural enough; but it is going to ruin my life, to turn me into a beast instead of a man. Good God! do you think I don't know what that woman will do for me? She will drag me down, down, down, to her own level. All my ideas, all my ambition, all my life's work will be bartered for a smug practice, among paying patients. I shall scheme and plot to make a big income that we may live like a couple of plump animals, that we may dress ourselves gaudily and parade our wealth. Nothing will satisfy her. Such women are leeches; their only cry is 'give, give, give.' So long as I can supply her with money she will tolerate me, and to get it for her I shall sell my heart, and my brain, and my soul. She will load herself with jewels, and go about from house to house, half naked, to leer at every man she comes across: that is 'life' to such women. And I shall trot behind her, the laughing stock of every fool, the contempt of every man."

His vehemence made any words I could say sound weak before they were uttered. What argument could I show stronger than that he had already put before himself? I knew his answer to everything I could urge.

My mistake had been in imagining him different from other men. I began to see that he was like the rest of us: part angel, part devil. But the new point he revealed to me was that the higher the one, the lower the other. It seems as if nature must balance her work; the nearer the leaves to heaven, the deeper the roots striking down into the darkness. I knew that his passion for this woman made no change in his truer love. The one was a spiritual, the other a mere animal passion. The memory of incidents that had puzzled me came back to enlighten me. I remembered how often on nights when I had sat up late, working, I had heard his steps pass my door, heavy and uncertain; how once in a dingy quarter of London, I had met one who had strangely resembled him. I had followed him to speak, but the man's bleared eyes had stared angrily at me, and I had turned away, calling myself a fool for my mistake. But as I looked at the face beside me now, I understood.

And then there rose up before my eyes the face I knew better, the eager noble face that to merely look upon had been good. We had reached a small, evil-smelling street, leading from Leicester Square towards Holborn. I caught him by the shoulders and turned him round with his back against some church railings. I forget what I said. We are strange mixtures. I thought of the shy, backward boy I had coached and bullied at old Fauerberg's, of the laughing handsome lad I had watched grow into manhood. The very restaurant we had most frequented in his old Oxford days — where we had poured out our souls to one another, was in this very street where we were standing. For the moment I felt towards him as perhaps his mother might have felt; I wanted to scold him and to cry with him; to shake him and to put my arms about him. I pleaded with him, and urged him, and called him every name I could put my tongue to. It must have seemed an odd conversation. A passing policeman, making a not unnatural mistake, turned his bull's-eye upon us, and advised us sternly to go home. We laughed, and with that laugh

Cyril came back to his own self, and we walked on to Staple Inn more soberly. He promised me to go away by the very first train the next morning, and to travel for some four or five months, and I undertook to make all the necessary explanations for him.

We both felt better for our talk, and when I wished him good-night at his door, it was the real Cyril Harjohn whose hand I gripped — the real Cyril, because the best that is in a man is his real self. If there be any future for man beyond this world, it is the good that is in him that will live. The other side of him is of the earth; it is that he will leave behind him.

He kept his word. In the morning he was gone, and I never saw him again. I had many letters from him, hopeful at first, full of strong resolves. He told me he had written to Elspeth, not telling her everything, for that she would not understand, but so much as would explain; and from her he had had sweet womanly letters in reply. I feared she might have been cold and unsympathetic, for often good women, untouched by temptation themselves, have small tenderness for those who struggle. But her goodness was something more than a mere passive quantity; she loved him the better because he had need of her. I believe she would have saved him from himself, had not fate interfered and taken the matter out of her hands. Women are capable of big sacrifices; I think this woman would have been content to lower herself, if by so doing she could have raised him.

But it was not to be. From India he wrote to me that he was coming home. I had not met the Fawley woman for some time, and she had gone out of my mind until one day, chancing upon a theatrical paper, some weeks old, I read that "Miss Fawley had sailed for Calcutta to fulfil an engagement of long standing."

I had his last letter in my pocket. I sat down and worked out the question of date. She would arrive in Calcutta the day before he left. Whether it was chance or intention on her part I never knew; as likely as not the former, for there is a fatalism in this world shaping our ends.

I heard no more from him, I hardly expected to do so, but three months later a mutual acquaintance stopped me on the Club steps.

"Have you heard the news," he said, "about young Harjohn?"

"No," I replied. "Is he married?"

"Married," he answered, "No, poor devil, he's dead!"

"Thank God," was on my lips, but fortunately I checked myself. "How did it happen?" I asked.

"At a shooting party, up at some Rajah's place. Must have caught his gun in some brambles, I suppose. The bullet went clean through his head."

"Dear me," I said, "how very sad!" I could think of nothing else to say at the moment.

THE MATERIALISATION OF CHARLES AND MIVANWAY

The fault that most people will find with this story is that it is unconvincing. Its scheme is improbable, its atmosphere artificial. To confess that the thing really happened — not as I am about to set it down, for the pen of the professional writer cannot but adorn and embroider, even to the detriment of his material — is, I am well aware, only an aggravation of my offence, for the facts of life are the impossibilities of fiction. A truer artist would have left this story alone, or at most have kept it for the irritation of his private circle. My lower instinct is to make use of it. A very old man told me the tale. He was landlord of the Cromlech Arms, the only inn of a small, rock-sheltered village on the north-east coast of Cornwall, and had been so for nine and forty years. It is called the Cromlech Hotel now, and is under new management, and during the season some four coach-loads of tourists sit down each day to *table d'hôte* lunch in the low-ceilinged parlour. But I am speaking of years ago, when the place was a mere fishing harbour, undiscovered by the guide books.

The old landlord talked, and I hearkened the while we both sat drinking thin ale from earthenware mugs, late one summer's evening, on the bench that runs along the wall just beneath the latticed windows. And during the many pauses, when the old landlord stopped to puff his pipe in silence, and lay in a new stock of breath, there came to us the murmuring voices of the Atlantic; and often, mingled with the pompous roar of the big breakers farther out, we would hear the rippling laugh of some small wave that, maybe, had crept in to listen to the tale the landlord told.

The mistake that Charles Seabohn, Junior partner of the firm of Seabohn & Son, civil engineers of London and Newcastle-upon-Tyne, and Mivanway Evans, youngest daughter of the Rev. Thomas Evans, Pastor of the Presbyterian Church at Bristol, made originally, was marrying too young. Charles Seabohn could hardly have been twenty years of age, and Mivanway could have been little more than seventeen, when they first met upon the cliffs, two miles beyond the Cromlech Arms. Young Charles Seabohn, coming across the village in the course of a walking tour, had decided to spend a day or two exploring the picturesque coast, and Mivanway's father had hired that year a neighbouring farmhouse wherein to spend his summer vacation.

Early one morning — for at twenty one is virtuous, and takes exercise before breakfast — as young Charles Seabohn lay upon the cliffs, watching the white waters coming and going upon the black rocks below, he became aware of a form rising from the waves. The figure was too far off for him to see it clearly, but judging from the costume, it was a female figure, and promptly the mind of Charles, poetically inclined, turned to thoughts of Venus — or Aphrodite, as he, being a gentleman of delicate taste would have preferred to term her. He saw the figure disappear behind a head-land, but still waited. In about ten minutes or a quarter of an hour it reappeared, clothed in the garments of the eighteen-sixties, and came towards him. Hidden from sight himself behind a group of rocks, he could watch it at his leisure, ascending the steep path from the beach, and an exceedingly sweet and dainty figure it would have appeared, even to eyes less susceptible than those of twenty. Sea-water — I stand open to correction — is not, I believe, considered anything of a substitute for curling tongs, but to the hair of the youngest Miss Evans it had given an additional and most fascinating wave. Nature's red and white had been most cunningly laid on, and the large childish eyes seemed to be searching the world for laughter, with which to feed a pair of delicious, pouting lips. Charles's upturned face, petrified into admiration, was just the sort of thing for which they were on the look-out. A startled "Oh!" came from the slightly parted lips, followed by the merriest of laughs, which in its turn was suddenly stopped by a deep blush. Then the youngest Miss Evans looked offended, as though the whole affair had been Charles's fault, which is the way of women. And Charles, feeling himself guilty under that stern gaze of indignation, rose awkwardly and apologised meekly, whether for being on the cliffs at all or for having got up too early, he would have been unable to explain.

The youngest Miss Evans graciously accepted the apology thus tendered with a bow, and passed on, and Charles stood staring after her till the valley gathered her into its spreading arms and hid her from his view.

That was the beginning of all things. I am speaking of the Universe as viewed from the standpoint of Charles and Mivanway.

Six months later they were man and wife, or perhaps it would be more correct to say boy and wifelet. Seabohn senior counselled delay, but was overruled by the impatience of his junior partner. The Reverend Mr. Evans, in common with most theologians, possessed a goodly supply of unmarried daughters, and a limited income. Personally he saw no necessity for postponement of the marriage.

The month's honeymoon was spent in the New Forest. That

was a mistake to begin with. The New Forest in February is depressing, and they had chosen the loneliest spot they could find. A fortnight in Paris or Rome would have been more helpful. As yet they had nothing to talk about except love, and that they had been talking and writing about steadily all through the winter. On the tenth morning Charles yawned, and Mivanway had a quiet half-hour's cry about it in her own room. On the sixteenth evening, Mivanway, feeling irritable, and wondering why (as though fifteen damp, chilly days in the New Forest were not sufficient to make any woman irritable), requested Charles not to disarrange her hair; and Charles, speechless with astonishment, went out into the garden, and swore before all the stars that he would never caress Mivanway's hair again as long as he lived.

One supreme folly they had conspired to commit, even before the commencement of the honeymoon. Charles, after the manner of very young lovers, had earnestly requested Mivanway to impose upon him some task. He desired to do something great and noble to show his devotion. Dragons was the thing he had in mind, though he may not have been aware of it. Dragons also, no doubt, flitted through Mivanway's brain, but unfortunately for lovers the supply of dragons has lapsed. Mivanway, liking the conceit, however, thought over it, and then decided that Charles must give up smoking. She had discussed the matter with her favourite sister, and that was the only thing the girls could think of. Charles's face fell. He suggested some more Herculean labour, some sacrifice more worthy to lay at Mivanway's feet. But Mivanway had spoken. She might think of some other task, but the smoking prohibition would, in any case, remain. She dismissed the subject with a pretty *hauteur* that would have graced Marie Antoinette.

Thus tobacco, the good angel of all men, no longer came each day to teach Charles patience and amiability, and he fell into the ways of short temper and selfishness.

They took up their residence in a suburb of Newcastle, and this was also unfortunate for them, because there the society was scanty and middle-aged; and, in consequence, they had still to depend much upon their own resources. They knew little of life, less of each other, and nothing at all of themselves. Of course they quarrelled, and each quarrel left the wound a little more raw. No kindly, experienced friend was at hand to laugh at them. Mivanway would write down all her sorrows in a bulky diary, which made her feel worse; so that before she had written for ten minutes her pretty, unwise head would drop upon her dimpled arm, and the book — the proper place for which was behind the fire — would become damp with her tears; and Charles, his day's work done and the clerks gone, would linger in his dingy office and hatch trifles into troubles.

The end came one evening after dinner, when, in the heat of a silly squabble, Charles boxed Mivanway's ears. That was very ungentlemanly conduct, and he was heartily ashamed of himself the moment he had done it, which was right and proper for him to be. The only excuse to be urged on his behalf is that girls sufficiently pretty to have been spoilt from childhood by everyone about them can at times be intensely irritating. Mivanway rushed up to her room, and locked herself in. Charles flew after her to apologise, but only arrived in time to have the door slammed in his face.

It had only been the merest touch. A boy's muscles move quicker than his thoughts. But to Mivanway it was a blow. This was what it had come to! This was the end of a man's love!

She spent half the night writing in the precious diary, with the result that in the morning she came down feeling more bitter than she had gone up. Charles had walked the streets of Newcastle all night, and that had not done him any good. He met her with an apology combined with an excuse, which was bad tactics. Mivanway, of course, fastened upon the excuse, and the quarrel recommenced. She mentioned that she hated him; he hinted that she had never loved him, and she retorted that he had never loved her. Had there been anybody by to knock their heads together and suggest breakfast, the thing might have blown over, but the combined effect of a sleepless night and an empty stomach upon each proved disastrous. Their words came poisoned from their brains, and each believed they meant what they said. That afternoon Charles sailed from Hull, on a ship bound for the Cape, and that evening Mivanway arrived at the paternal home in Bristol with two trunks and the curt information that she and Charles had separated for ever. The next morning both thought of a soft speech to say to the other, but the next morning was just twenty-four hours too late.

Eight days afterwards Charles's ship was run down in a fog, near the coast of Portugal, and every soul on board was supposed to have perished. Mivanway read his name among the list of lost; the child died within her, and she knew herself for a woman who had loved deeply, and will not love again.

Good luck intervening, however, Charles and one other man were rescued by a small trading vessel, and landed in Algiers. There Charles learnt of his supposed death, and the idea occurred to him to leave the report uncontradicted. For one thing, it solved a problem that had been troubling him. He could trust his father to see to it that his own small fortune, with possibly something added, was handed over to Mivanway, and she would be free if she wished to marry again. He was convinced that she did not care for him, and that she had read of his death with a sense of relief. He would make a new life for himself, and forget her.

He continued his journey to the Cape, and once there he soon gained for himself an excellent position. The colony was young, engineers were welcome, and Charles knew his business. He found the life interesting and exciting. The rough, dangerous up-country work suited him, and the time passed swiftly.

But in thinking he would forget Mivanway, he had not taken into consideration his own character, which at bottom was a very gentlemanly character. Out on the lonely veldt he found himself dreaming of her. The memory of her pretty face and merry laugh came back to him at all hours. Occasionally he would curse her roundly, but that only meant that he was sore because of the thought of her; what he was really cursing was himself and his own folly. Softened by the distance, her quick temper, her very petulance became mere added graces; and if we consider women as human beings and not as angels, it was certainly a fact that he had lost a very sweet and lovable woman. Ah! if she only were by his side now — now that he was a man capable of appreciating her, and not a foolish, selfish boy. This thought would come to him as he sat smoking at the door of his tent, and then he would regret that the stars looking down upon him were not the same stars that were watching her, it would have made him feel nearer to her. For, though young people may not credit it, one grows more sentimental as one grows older; at least, some of us do, and they perhaps not the least wise.

One night he had a vivid dream of her. She came to him and held out her hand, and he took it, and they said good-bye to one another. They were standing on the cliff where he had first met her, and one of them was going upon a long journey, though he was not sure which.

In the towns men laugh at dreams, but away from civilisation we listen more readily to the strange tales that Nature whispers to us. Charles Seabohn recollected this dream when he awoke in the morning.

"She is dying," he said, "and she has come to wish me good-bye."

He made up his mind to return to England at once; perhaps if he made haste he would be in time to kiss her. But he could not start that day, for work was to be done; and Charles Seabohn, lover though he still was, had grown to be a man, and knew that work must not be neglected even though the heart may be calling. So for a day or two he stayed, and on the third night he dreamed of Mivanway again, and this time she lay within the little chapel at Bristol where, on Sunday mornings, he had often sat with her. He heard her father's voice reading the burial service over her, and the sister she had loved best was sitting beside him, crying softly. Then Charles knew that there was no need for him to hasten. So he remained to finish his work. That done, he would return to England. He would like again to stand upon the cliffs, above the little Cornish village, where they had first met.

Thus a few months later Charles Seabohn, or Charles Denning, as he called himself, aged and bronzed, not easily recognisable by those who had not known him well, walked into the Cromlech Arms, as six years before he had walked in with his knapsack on his back, and asked for a room, saying he would be stopping in the village for a short while.

In the evening he strolled out and made his way to the cliffs. It was twilight when he reached the place of rocks to which the fancy-loving Cornish folk had given the name of the Witches' Cauldron. It was from this spot that he had first watched Mivanway coming to him from the sea.

He took the pipe from his mouth, and leaning against a rock, whose rugged outline seemed fashioned into the face of an old friend, gazed down the narrow pathway now growing indistinct in the dim light. And as he gazed the figure of Mivanway came slowly up the pathway from the sea, and paused before him.

He felt no fear. He had half expected it. Her coming was the complement of his dreams. She looked older and graver than he remembered her, but for that the face was the sweeter.

He wondered if she would speak to him, but she only looked at him with sad eyes; and he stood there in the shadow of the rocks without moving, and she passed on into the twilight.

Had he on his return cared to discuss the subject with his landlord, had he even shown himself a ready listener — for the old man loved to gossip — he might have learnt that a young widow lady named Mrs. Charles Seabohn, accompanied by an unmarried sister, had lately come to reside in the neighbourhood, having, upon the death of a former tenant, taken the lease of a small farmhouse sheltered in the valley a mile beyond the village, and that her favourite evening's walk was to the sea and back by the steep footway leading past the Witches' Cauldron.

Had he followed the figure of Mivanway into the valley, he would have known that out of sight of the Witches' Cauldron it took to running fast till it reached a welcome door, and fell panting into the arms of another figure that had hastened out to meet it.

"My dear," said the elder woman, "you are trembling like a leaf. What has happened?"

"I have seen him," answered Mivanway.

"Seen whom?"

"Charles."

"Charles!" repeated the other, looking at Mivanway as though she thought her mad.

"His spirit, I mean," explained Mivanway, in an awed voice. "It was standing in the shadow of the rocks, in the exact spot where we first met. It looked older and more careworn; but, oh! Margaret, so sad and reproachful."

"My dear," said her sister, leading her in, "you are overwrought. I wish we had never come back to this house."

"Oh! I was not frightened," answered Mivanway, "I have been expecting it every evening. I am so glad it came. Perhaps it will come again, and I can ask it to forgive me."

So next night Mivanway, though much against her sister's wishes and advice, persisted in her usual walk, and Charles at the same twilight hour started from the inn.

Again Mivanway saw him standing in the shadow of the rocks. Charles had made up his mind that if the thing happened again he would speak, but when the silent figure of Mivanway, clothed in the fading light, stopped and gazed at him, his will failed him.

That it was the spirit of Mivanway standing before him he had not the faintest doubt. One may dismiss other people's ghosts as the phantasies of a weak brain, but one knows one's own to be realities, and Charles for the last five years had mingled with a people whose dead dwell about them. Once, drawing his courage around him, he made to speak, but as he did so the figure of Mivanway shrank from him, and only a sigh escaped his lips, and hearing that the figure of Mivanway turned and again passed down the path into the valley, leaving Charles gazing after it.

But the third night both arrived at the trysting spot with determination screwed up to the sticking point.

Charles was the first to speak. As the figure of Mivanway came towards him, with its eyes fixed sadly on him, he moved from the shadow of the rocks, and stood before it.

"Mivanway!" he said.

"Charles!" replied the figure of Mivanway. Both spoke in an awed whisper suitable to the circumstances, and each stood gazing sorrowfully upon the other.

"Are you happy?" asked Mivanway.

The question strikes one as somewhat farcical, but it must be remembered that Mivanway was the daughter of a Gospeller of the old school, and had been brought up to beliefs that were not then out of date.

"As happy as I deserve to be," was the sad reply, and the answer — the inference was not complimentary to Charles's deserts — struck a chill to Mivanway's heart.

"How could I be happy having lost you?" went on the voice of Charles.

Now this speech fell very pleasantly upon Mivanway's ears. In the first place it relieved her of her despair regarding Charles's future. No doubt his present suffering was keen, but there was hope for him. Secondly, it was a decidedly "pretty" speech for a ghost, and I am not at all sure that Mivanway was the kind of woman to be averse to a little mild flirtation with the spirit of Charles.

"Can you forgive me?" asked Mivanway.

"Forgive *you*!" replied Charles, in a tone of awed astonishment. "Can you forgive me? I was a brute — a fool — I was not worthy to love you."

A most gentlemanly spirit it seemed to be. Mivanway forgot to be afraid of it.

"We were both to blame," answered Mivanway. But this time there was less submission in her tones. "But I was the most at fault. I was a petulant child. I did not know how deeply I loved you."

"You loved me!" repeated the voice of Charles, and the voice lingered over the words as though it found them sweet.

"Surely you never doubted it," answered the voice of Mivanway. "I never ceased to love you. I shall love you always and ever."

The figure of Charles sprang forward as though it would clasp the ghost of Mivanway in its arms, but halted a step or two off.

"Bless me before you go," he said, and with uncovered head the figure of Charles knelt to the figure of Mivanway.

Really, ghosts could be exceedingly nice when they liked. Mivanway bent graciously towards her shadowy suppliant, and, as she did so, her eye caught sight of something on the grass beside it, and that something was a well-coloured meerschaum pipe. There was no mistaking it for anything else, even in that treacherous light; it lay glistening where Charles, in falling upon his knees had jerked it from his breast-pocket.

Charles, following Mivanway's eyes, saw it also, and the memory of the prohibition against smoking came back to him.

Without stopping to consider the futility of the action — nay, the direct confession implied thereby — he instinctively grabbed at the pipe, and rammed it back into his pocket; and then an avalanche of mingled understanding and bewilderment, fear and joy, swept Mivanway's brain before it. She felt she must do one of two things, laugh or scream and go on screaming, and she laughed. Peal after peal of laughter she sent echoing among the rocks, and Charles springing to his feet was just in time to catch her as she fell forward a dead weight into his arms.

Ten minutes later the eldest Miss Evans, hearing heavy foot-steps, went to the door. She saw what she took to be the spirit of Charles Seabohn, staggering under the weight of the lifeless body of Mivanway, and the sight not unnaturally alarmed her. Charles's suggestion of brandy, however, sounded human, and the urgent need of attending to Mivanway kept her mind from dwelling upon problems tending towards insanity.

Charles carried Mivanway to her room, and laid her upon the bed.

"I'll leave her with you," he whispered to the eldest Miss Evans. "It will be better for her not to see me until she is quite recovered. She has had a shock."

Charles waited in the dark parlour for what seemed to him an exceedingly long time. But at last the eldest Miss Evans returned.

"She's all right now," were the welcome words he heard.

"I'll go and see her," he said.

"But she's in bed," exclaimed the scandalised Miss Evans.

And then as Charles only laughed, "Oh, ah — yes, I suppose — of course," she added.

And the eldest Miss Evans, left alone, sat down and wrestled with the conviction that she was dreaming.

PORTRAIT OF A LADY

My work pressed upon me, but the louder it challenged me — such is the heart of the timid fighter — the less stomach I felt for the contest. I wrestled with it in my study, only to be driven to my books. I walked out to meet it in the streets, only to seek shelter from it in music-hall or theatre. Thereupon it waxed importunate and over-bearing, till the shadow of it darkened all my doings. The thought of it sat beside me at the table, and spoilt my appetite. The memory of it followed me abroad, and stood between me and my friends, so that all talk died upon my lips, and I moved among men as one ghost-ridden.

Then the throbbing town, with its thousand distracting voices, grew maddening to me. I felt the need of converse with solitude, that master and teacher of all the arts, and I bethought me of the Yorkshire Wolds, where a man may walk all day, meeting no human creature, hearing no voice but the curlew's cry; where, lying prone upon the sweet grass, he may feel the pulsation of the earth, travel-ling at its eleven hundred miles a minute through the ether. So one morning I bundled many things, some needful, more needless, into a bag, hurrying lest somebody or something should happen to stay me, and that night I lay in a small northern town that stands upon the borders of smokedom at the gate of the great moors; and at seven the next morning I took my seat beside a one-eyed carrier behind an ancient piebald mare. The one-eyed carrier cracked his whip, the piebald horse jogged forward. The nineteenth century, with its turmoil, fell away behind us; the distant hills, creeping nearer, swallowed us up, and we became but a moving speck upon the face of the quiet earth.

Late in the afternoon we arrived at a village, the memory of which had been growing in my mind. It lies in the triangle formed by the sloping walls of three great fells, and not even the telegraph wire has reached it yet, to murmur to it whispers of the restless world — or had not at the time of which I write. Nought disturbs it save, once a day, the one-eyed carrier — if he and his piebald mare have not yet laid their ancient bones to rest — who, passing through, leaves a few letters and parcels to be called for by the people of the scattered hill-farms round about. It is the meeting-place of two noisy brooks. Through the sleepy days and the hushed nights, one hears them ever chattering to themselves as children playing alone some game of make-believe. Coming from their far-off homes among the hills, they mingle their waters here, and journey on in company, and then their converse is more serious, as becomes those who have joined hands and are moving onward towards life together. Later they reach sad, weary towns, black beneath a never-lifted pall of smoke, where day and night the clang of iron drowns all human voices, where the children play with ashes, where the men and women have dull, patient faces; and so on, muddy and stained, to the deep sea that ceaselessly calls to them. Here, however, their waters are fresh and clear, and their passing makes the only stir that the valley has ever known. Surely, of all peaceful places, this was the one where a tired worker might find strength.

My one-eyed friend had suggested I should seek lodgings at the house of one Mistress Cholmondley, a widow lady, who resided with her only daughter in the white-washed cottage that is the last house in the village, if you take the road that leads over Coll Fell.

"Tha' can see th' house from here, by reason o' its standing so high above t'others," said the carrier, pointing with his whip. "It's theer or nowhere, aw'm thinking, for folks don't often coom seeking lodgings in these parts."

The tiny dwelling, half smothered in June roses, looked idyllic, and after a lunch of bread and cheese at the little inn I made my way to it by the path that passes through the churchyard. I had conjured up the vision of a stout, pleasant, comfort-radiating woman, assisted by some bright, fresh girl, whose rosy cheeks and sunburnt hands would help me banish from my mind all clogging recollections of the town; and hopeful, I pushed back the half-opened door and entered.

The cottage was furnished with a taste that surprised me, but in themselves my hosts disappointed me. My bustling, comely housewife turned out a wizened, blear-eyed dame. All day long she dozed in her big chair, or crouched with shrivelled hands spread out before the fire. My dream of winsome maidenhood vanished before the reality of a weary-looking, sharp-featured woman of between forty and fifty. Perhaps there had been a time when the listless eyes had sparkled with roguish merriment, when the shrivelled, tight-drawn lips had pouted temptingly; but spinsterhood does not sweeten the juices of a woman, and strong country air, though, like old ale, it is good when taken occasionally, dulls the brain if lived upon. A narrow, uninteresting woman I found her, troubled with a shyness that sat ludicrously upon her age, and that yet failed to save her from the landlady's customary failing of loquacity concerning "better days," together with an irritating, if harmless, affectation of youthfulness.

All other details were, however, most satisfactory; and at the window commanding the road that leads through the valley towards the distant world I settled down to face my work.

But the spirit of industry, once driven forth, returns with coy steps. I wrote for perhaps an hour, and then throwing down my halting pen I looked about the room, seeking distraction. A Chippendale book-case stood against the wall and I strolled over to it. The key was in the lock, and opening its glass doors, I examined the well-filled shelves. They held a curious collection: miscellanies with quaint, glazed bindings; novels and poems; whose authors I had never heard of; old magazines long dead, their very names forgotten; "keepsakes" and annuals, redolent of an age of vastly pretty sentiments and lavender-coloured silks. On the top shelf, however, was a volume of Keats wedged between a number of the *Evangelical Rambler* and Young's *Night Thoughts*, and standing on tip-toe, I sought to draw it from its place.

The book was jambed so tightly that my efforts brought two or three others tumbling about me, covering me with a cloud of fine dust, and to my feet there fell, with a rattle of glass and metal, a small miniature painting, framed in black wood.

I picked it up, and, taking it to the window, examined it. It was the picture of a young girl, dressed in the fashion of thirty years ago — I mean thirty years ago then. I fear it must be nearer fifty, speaking as from now — when our grandmothers wore corkscrew curls, and low-cut bodices that one wonders how they kept from slipping down. The face was beautiful, not merely with the conventional beauty of tiresome regularity and impossible colouring such as one finds in all miniatures, but with soul behind the soft deep eyes. As I gazed, the sweet lips seemed to laugh at me, and yet there lurked a sadness in the smile, as though the artist, in some rare moment, had seen the coming shadow of life across the sunshine of the face. Even my small knowledge of Art told me that the work was clever, and I wondered why it should have lain so long neglected, when as a mere ornament it was valuable. It must have been placed in the book-case years ago by someone, and forgotten.

I replaced it among its dusty companions, and sat down once more to my work. But between me and the fading light came the face of the miniature, and would not be banished. Wherever I turned it looked out at me from the shadows. I am not naturally fanciful, and the work I was engaged upon — the writing of a farcical comedy — was not of the kind to excite the dreamy side of a man's nature. I grew angry with myself, and made a further effort to fix my mind upon the paper in front of me. But my thoughts refused to return from their wanderings. Once, glancing back over my shoulder, I could have sworn I saw the original of the picture sitting in the big chintz-covered chair in the far corner. It was dressed in a faded lilac frock, trimmed with some old lace, and I could not help noticing the beauty of the folded hands, though in the portrait only the head and shoulders had been drawn.

Next morning I had forgotten the incident, but with the lighting of the lamp the memory of it awoke within me, and my interest grew so strong that again I took the miniature from its hiding-place and looked at it.

And then the knowledge suddenly came to me that I knew the face. Where had I seen her, and when? I had met her and spoken to her. The picture smiled at me, as if rallying me on my forgetfulness. I put it back upon its shelf, and sat racking my brains trying to recollect. We had met somewhere — in the country — a long time ago, and had talked of common-place things. To the vision of her clung the scent of roses and the murmuring voices of haymakers. Why had I never seen her again? Why had she passed so completely out of my mind?

My landlady entered to lay my supper, and I questioned her assuming a careless tone. Reason with or laugh at myself as I would, this shadowy memory was becoming a romance to me. It was as though I were talking of some loved, dead friend, even to speak of whom to commonplace people was a sacrilege. I did not want the woman to question me in return.

"Oh, yes," answered my landlady. Ladies had often lodged with her. Sometimes people stayed the whole summer, wandering about the woods and fells, but to her thinking the great hills were lonesome. Some of her lodgers had been young ladies, but she could not remember any of them having impressed her with their beauty. But then it was said women were never a judge of other women. They had come and gone. Few had ever returned, and fresh faces drove out the old.

"You have been letting lodgings for a long time?" I asked. "I suppose it could be fifteen — twenty years ago that strangers to you lived in this room?"

"Longer than that," she said quietly, dropping for the moment all affectation. "We came here from the farm when my father died. He had had losses, and there was but little left. That is twenty-seven years ago now."

I hastened to close the conversation, fearing long-winded recollections of "better days." I have heard such so often from one landlady and another. I had not learnt much. Who was the original of the miniature, how it came to be lying forgotten in the dusty book-case were still mysteries; and with a strange perversity I could not have explained to myself I shrank from putting a direct question.

So two days more passed by. My work took gradually a firmer grip upon my mind, and the face of the miniature visited me less often. But in the evening of the third day, which was a Sunday, a curious thing happened.

I was returning from a stroll, and dusk was falling as I reached the cottage. I had been thinking of my farce, and I was laughing to myself at a situation that seemed to me comical, when, passing the window of my room, I saw looking out the sweet fair face that had become so familiar to me. It stood close to the latticed panes, a slim, girlish figure, clad in the old-fashioned lilac-coloured frock in which I had imagined it on the first night of my arrival, the beautiful hands clasped across the breast, as then they had been folded on the lap. Her eyes were gazing down the road that passes through the village and goes south, but they seemed to be dreaming, not seeing, and the sadness in them struck upon one almost as a cry. I was close to the window, but the hedge screened me, and I remained watching, until, after a minute I suppose, though it appeared longer, the figure drew back into the darkness of the room and disappeared.

I entered, but the room was empty. I called, but no one answered. The uncomfortable suggestion took hold of me that I must be growing a little crazy. All that had gone before I could explain to myself as a mere train of thought, but this time it had come to me suddenly, uninvited, while my thoughts had been busy elsewhere. This thing had appeared not to my brain but to my senses. I am not a believer in ghosts, but I am in the hallucinations of a weak mind, and my own explanation was in consequence not very satisfactory to myself.

I tried to dismiss the incident, but it would not leave me, and later that same evening something else occurred that fixed it still clearer in my thoughts. I had taken out two or three books at random with which to amuse myself, and turning over the leaves of one of them, a volume of verses by some obscure poet, I found its sentimental passages much scored and commented upon in pencil as was common fifty years ago — as may be common now, for your Fleet Street cynic has not altered the world and its ways to quite the extent that he imagines.

One poem in particular had evidently appealed greatly to the reader's sympathies. It was the old, old story of the gallant who woos and rides away, leaving the maiden to weep. The poetry was poor, and at another time its conventionality would have excited only my ridicule. But, reading it in conjunction with the quaint, naive notes scattered about its margins, I felt no inclination to jeer. These hackneyed stories that we laugh at are deep profundities to the many who find in them some shadow of their own sorrows, and she — for it was a woman's handwriting — to whom this book belonged had loved its trite verses, because in them she had read her own heart. This, I told myself, was her story also. A common enough story in life as in literature, but novel to those who live it.

There was no reason for my connecting her with the original of the miniature, except perhaps a subtle relationship between the thin nervous handwriting and the mobile features; yet I felt instinctively they were one and the same, and that I was tracing, link by link, the history of my forgotten friend.

I felt urged to probe further, and next morning while my landlady was clearing away my breakfast things, I fenced round the subject once again.

"By the way," I said, "while I think of it, if I leave any books or papers here behind me, send them on at once. I have a knack of doing that sort of thing. I suppose," I added, "your lodgers often do leave some of their belongings behind them."

It sounded to myself a clumsy ruse. I wondered if she would suspect what was behind it.

"Not often," she answered. "Never that I can remember, except in the case of one poor lady who died here."

I glanced up quickly.

"In this room?" I asked.

My landlady seemed troubled at my tone.

"Well, not exactly in this very room. We carried her upstairs, but she died immediately. She was dying when she came here. I should not have taken her in had I known. So many people are prejudiced against a house where death has occurred, as if there were anywhere it had not. It was not quite fair to us."

I did not speak for a while, and the rattle of the plates and knives continued undisturbed.

"What did she leave here?" I asked at length.

"Oh, just a few books and photographs, and such-like small things that people bring with them to lodgings," was the reply. "Her people promised to send for them, but they never did, and I suppose I forgot them. They were not of any value."

The woman turned as she was leaving the room.

"It won't drive you away, sir, I hope, what I have told you," she said. "It all happened a long while ago.

"Of course not," I answered. "It interested me, that was all." And the woman went out, closing the door behind her.

So here was the explanation, if I chose to accept it. I sat long that morning, wondering to myself whether things I had learnt to laugh at could be after all realities. And a day or two afterwards I made a discovery that confirmed all my vague surmises.

Rummaging through this same dusty book-case, I found in one of the ill-fitting drawers, beneath a heap of torn and tumbled books, a diary belonging to the fifties, stuffed with many letters and shapeless flowers, pressed between stained pages; and there — for the writer of stories, tempted by human documents, is weak — in faded ink, brown and withered like the flowers, I read the story I already knew.

Such a very old story it was, and so conventional. He was an artist — was ever story of this type written where the hero was not an artist? They had been children together, loving each other without knowing it till one day it was revealed to them. Here is the entry: —

"May 18th. — I do not know what to say, or how to begin. Chris loves me. I have been praying to God to make me worthy of him, and dancing round the room in my bare feet for fear of waking them below. He kissed my hands and clasped them round his neck, saying they were beautiful as the hands of a goddess, and he knelt and kissed them again. I am holding them before me and kissing them myself. I am glad they are so beautiful. O God, why are you so good to me? Help me to be a true wife to him. Help me that I may never give him an instant's pain! Oh, that I had more power of loving, that I might love him better," — and thus foolish thoughts for many pages, but foolish thoughts of the kind that has kept this worn old world, hanging for so many ages in space, from turning sour.

Later, in February, there is another entry that carries on the story: —

"Chris left this morning. He put a little packet into my hands at the last moment, saying it was the most precious thing he possessed, and that when I looked at it I was to think of him who loved it. Of course I guessed what it was, but I did not open it till I was alone in my room. It is the picture of myself that he has been so secret about, but oh, so beautiful. I wonder if I am really as beautiful as this. But I wish he had not made me look so sad. I am kissing the little lips. I love them, because he loved to kiss them. Oh, sweetheart! it will be long before you kiss them again. Of course it was right for him to go, and I am glad he has been able to manage it. He could not study properly in this quiet country place, and now he will be able to go to Paris and Rome and he will be great. Even the stupid people here see how clever he is. But, oh, it will be so long before I see him again, my love! my king!"

With each letter that comes from him, similar foolish rhapsodies are written down, but these letters of his, I gather, as I turn the pages, grow after a while colder and fewer, and a chill fear that dare not be penned creeps in among the words.

"March 12th. Six weeks and no letter from Chris, and, oh dear! I am so hungry for one, for the last I have almost kissed to pieces. I suppose he will write more often when he gets to London. He is working hard, I know, and it is selfish of me to expect him to write more often, but I would sit up all night for a week rather than miss writing to him. I suppose men are not like that. O God, help me, help me, whatever happens! How foolish I am to-night! He was always careless. I will punish him for it when he comes back, but not very much."

Truly enough a conventional story.

Letters do come from him after that, but apparently they are less and less satisfactory, for the diary grows angry and bitter, and the faded writing is blotted at times with tears. Then towards the end of another year there comes this entry, written in a hand of strange neatness and precision: —

"It is all over now. I am glad it is finished. I have written to him, giving him up. I have told him I have ceased to care for him, and that it is better we should both be free. It is best that way. He would have had to ask me to release him, and that would have given him pain. He was always gentle. Now he will be able to marry her with an easy conscience, and he need never know what I have suffered. She is more fitted for him than I am. I hope he will be happy. I think I have done the right thing."

A few lines follow, left blank, and then the writing is resumed, but in a stronger, more vehement hand.

"Why do I lie to myself? I hate her! I would kill her if I could. I hope she will make him wretched, and that he will come to hate her as I do, and that she will die! Why did I let them persuade me to send that lying letter? He will show it to her, and she will see through it and laugh at me. I could have held him to his promise; he could not have got out of it.

"What do I care about dignity, and womanliness, and right, and all the rest of the canting words! I want him. I want his kisses and his arms about me. He is mine! He loved me once! I have only given him up because I thought it a fine thing to play the saint. It is only an acted lie. I would rather be evil, and he loved me. Why do I deceive myself? I want him. I care for nothing else at the bottom of my heart — his love, his kisses!"

And towards the end. "My God, what am I saying? Have I no shame, no strength? O God, help me!"

And there the diary closes.

I looked among the letters lying between the pages of the book. Most of them were signed simply "Chris." or "Christopher." But one gave his name in full, and it was a name I know well as that of a famous man, whose hand I have often shaken. I thought of his hard-featured, handsome wife, and of his great chill place, half house, half exhibition, in Kensington, filled constantly with its smart, chattering set, among whom he seemed always to be the uninvited guest; of his weary face and bitter tongue. And thinking thus there rose up before me the sweet, sad face of the woman of the miniature, and, meeting her eyes as she smiled at me from out of the shadows, I looked at her my wonder.

I took the miniature from its shelf. There would be no harm now in learning her name. So I stood with it in my hand till a little later my landlady entered to lay the cloth.

"I tumbled this out of your book-case," I said, "in reaching down some books. It is someone I know, someone I have met, but I cannot think where. Do you know who it is?"

The woman took it from my hand, and a faint flush crossed her withered face. "I had lost it," she answered. "I never thought of looking there. It's a portrait of myself, painted years ago, by a friend."

I looked from her to the miniature, as she stood among the shadows, with the lamplight falling on her face, and saw her perhaps for the first time.

"How stupid of me," I answered. "Yes, I see the likeness now."

THE MAN WHO
WOULD MANAGE

It has been told me by those in a position to know — and I can believe it — that at nineteen months of age he wept because his grandmother would not allow him to feed her with a spoon, and that at three and a half he was fished, in an exhausted condition, out of the water-butt, whither he had climbed for the purpose of teaching a frog to swim.

Two years later he permanently injured his left eye, showing the cat how to carry kittens without hurting them, and about the same period was dangerously stung by a bee while conveying it from a flower where, as it seemed to him, it was only wasting its time, to one more rich in honey-making properties.

His desire was always to help others. He would spend whole mornings explaining to elderly hens how to hatch eggs, and would give up an afternoon's black-berrying to sit at home and crack nuts for his pet squirrel. Before he was seven he would argue with his mother upon the management of children, and reprove his father for the way he was bringing him up.

As a child nothing could afford him greater delight than "minding" other children, or them less. He would take upon himself this harassing duty entirely of his own accord, without hope of reward or gratitude. It was immaterial to him whether the other children were older than himself or younger, stronger or weaker, whenever and wherever he found them he set to work to "mind" them. Once, during a school treat, piteous cries were heard coming from a distant part of the wood, and upon search being made, he was discovered prone upon the ground, with a cousin of his, a boy twice his own weight, sitting upon him and steadily whacking him. Having rescued him, the teacher said:

"Why don't you keep with the little boys? What are you doing along with him?"

"Please, sir," was the answer, "I was minding him."

He would have "minded" Noah if he had got hold of him.

He was a good-natured lad, and at school he was always willing for the whole class to copy from his slate — indeed he would urge them to do so. He meant it kindly, but inasmuch as his answers were invariably quite wrong — with a distinctive and inimitable wrongness peculiar to himself — the result to his followers was eminently unsatisfactory; and with the shallowness of youth that, ignoring motives, judges solely from results, they would wait for him outside and punch him.

All his energies went to the instruction of others, leaving none for his own purposes. He would take callow youths to his chambers and teach them to box.

"Now, try and hit me on the nose," he would say, standing before them in an attitude of defence. "Don't be afraid. Hit as hard as ever you can."

And they would do it. And so soon as he had recovered from his surprise, and a little lessened the bleeding, he would explain to them how they had done it all wrong, and how easily he could have stopped the blow if they had only hit him properly.

Twice at golf he lamed himself for over a week, showing a novice how to "drive"; and at cricket on one occasion I remember seeing his middle stump go down like a ninepin just as he was explaining to the bowler how to get the balls in straight. After which he had a long argument with the umpire as to whether he was in or out.

He has been known, during a stormy Channel passage, to rush excitedly upon the bridge in order to inform the captain that he had "just seen a light about two miles away to the left"; and if he is on the top of an omnibus he generally sits beside the driver, and points out to him the various obstacles likely to impede their progress.

It was upon an omnibus that my own personal acquaintance-ship with him began. I was sitting behind two ladies when the conductor came up to collect fares. One of them handed him a sixpence telling him to take to Piccadilly Circus, which was twopence.

"No," said the other lady to her friend, handing the man a shilling, "I owe you sixpence, you give me fourpence and I'll pay for the two."

The conductor took the shilling, punched two twopenny tickets, and then stood trying to think it out.

"That's right," said the lady who had spoken last, "give my friend fourpence."

The conductor did so.

"Now you give that fourpence to me."

The friend handed it to her.

"And you," she concluded to the conductor, "give me eightpence, then we shall be all right."

The conductor doled out to her the eightpence — the sixpence he had taken from the first lady, with a penny and two halfpennies out of his own bag — distrustfully, and retired, muttering something about his duties not including those of a lightning calculator.

"Now," said the elder lady to the younger, "I owe you a shilling."

I deemed the incident closed, when suddenly a florid gentleman on the opposite seat called out in stentorian tones: —

"Hi, conductor! you've cheated these ladies out of fourpence."

"'Oo's cheated 'oo out 'o fourpence?" replied the indignant conductor from the top of the steps, "it was a twopenny fare."

"Two twopences don't make eightpence," retorted the florid gentleman hotly. "How much did you give the fellow, my dear?" he asked, addressing the first of the young ladies.

"I gave him sixpence," replied the lady, examining her purse. "And then I gave you fourpence, you know," she added, addressing her companion.

"That's a dear two pen'oth," chimed in a common-looking man on the seat behind.

"Oh, that's impossible, dear," returned the other, "because I owed you sixpence to begin with."

"But I did," persisted the first lady.

"You gave me a shilling," said the conductor, who had returned, pointing an accusing forefinger at the elder of the ladies.

The elder lady nodded.

"And I gave you sixpence and two pennies, didn't I?"

The lady admitted it.

"An' I give 'er" — he pointed towards the younger lady — "fourpence, didn't I?"

"Which I gave you, you know, dear," remarked the younger lady.

"Blow me if it ain't *me* as 'as been cheated out of the fourpence," cried the conductor.

"But," said the florid gentleman, "the other lady gave you sixpence."

"Which I give to 'er," replied the conductor, again pointing the finger of accusation at the elder lady. "You can search my bag if yer like. I ain't got a bloomin' sixpence on me."

By this time everybody had forgotten what they had done, and contradicted themselves and one another. The florid man took it upon himself to put everybody right, with the result that before Piccadilly Circus was reached three passengers had threatened to report the conductor for unbecoming language. The conductor had called a policeman and had taken the names and addresses of the two ladies, intending to sue them for the fourpence (which they wanted to pay, but which the florid man would not allow them to do); the younger lady had become convinced that the elder lady had meant to cheat her, and the elder lady was in tears.

The florid gentleman and myself continued to Charing Cross

Station. At the booking office window it transpired that we were bound for the same suburb, and we journeyed down together. He talked about the fourpence all the way.

At my gate we shook hands, and he was good enough to express delight at the discovery that we were near neighbours. What attracted him to myself I failed to understand, for he had bored me considerably, and I had, to the best of my ability, snubbed him. Subsequently I learned that it was a peculiarity of his to be charmed with anyone who did not openly insult him.

Three days afterwards he burst into my study unannounced — he appeared to regard himself as my bosom friend — and asked me to forgive him for not having called sooner, which I did.

"I met the postman as I was coming along," he said, handing me a blue envelope, "and he gave me this, for you."

I saw it was an application for the water-rate.

"We must make a stand against this," he continued. "That's for water to the 29th September. You've no right to pay it in June."

I replied to the effect that water-rates had to be paid, and that it seemed to me immaterial whether they were paid in June or September.

"That's not it," he answered, "it's the principle of the thing. Why should you pay for water you have never had? What right have they to bully you into paying what you don't owe?"

He was a fluent talker, and I was ass enough to listen to him. By the end of half an hour he had persuaded me that the question was bound up with the inalienable rights of man, and that if I paid that fourteen and tenpence in June instead of in September, I should be unworthy of the privileges my forefathers had fought and died to bestow upon me.

He told me the company had not a leg to stand upon, and at his instigation I sat down and wrote an insulting letter to the chairman.

The secretary replied that, having regard to the attitude I had taken up, it would be incumbent upon themselves to treat it as a test case, and presumed that my solicitors would accept service on my behalf.

When I showed him this letter he was delighted.

"You leave it to me," he said, pocketing the correspondence, "and we'll teach them a lesson."

I left it to him. My only excuse is that at the time I was immersed in the writing of what in those days was termed a comedy-drama. The little sense I possessed must, I suppose, have been absorbed by the play.

The magistrate's decision somewhat damped my ardour, but

only inflamed his zeal. Magistrates, he said, were muddle-headed old fogies. This was a matter for a judge.

The judge was a kindly old gentleman, and said that bearing in mind the unsatisfactory wording of the sub-clause, he did not think he could allow the company their costs, so that, all told, I got off for something under fifty pounds, inclusive of the original fourteen and tenpence.

Afterwards our friendship waned, but living as we did in the same outlying suburb, I was bound to see a good deal of him; and to hear more.

At parties of all kinds he was particularly prominent, and on such occasions, being in his most good-natured mood, was most to be dreaded. No human being worked harder for the enjoyment of others, or produced more universal wretchedness.

One Christmas afternoon, calling upon a friend, I found some fourteen or fifteen elderly ladies and gentlemen trotting solemnly round a row of chairs in the centre of the drawing-room while Poppleton played the piano. Every now and then Poppleton would suddenly cease, and everyone would drop wearily into the nearest chair, evidently glad of a rest; all but one, who would thereupon creep quietly away, followed by the envying looks of those left behind. I stood by the door watching the weird scene. Presently an escaped player came towards me, and I enquired of him what the ceremony was supposed to signify.

"Don't ask me," he answered grumpily. "Some of Poppleton's damned tomfoolery." Then he added savagely, "We've got to play forfeits after this."

The servant was still waiting a favourable opportunity to announce me. I gave her a shilling not to, and got away unperceived.

After a satisfactory dinner, he would suggest an impromptu dance, and want you to roll up mats, or help him move the piano to the other end of the room.

He knew enough round games to have started a small purgatory of his own. Just as you were in the middle of an interesting discussion, or a delightful *tête-à-tête* with a pretty woman, he would swoop down upon you with: "Come along, we're going to play literary consequences," and dragging you to the table, and putting a piece of paper and a pencil before you, would tell you to write a description of your favourite heroine in fiction, and would see that you did it.

He never spared himself. It was always he who would volunteer to escort the old ladies to the station, and who would never leave them until he had seen them safely into the wrong train. He it was who would play "wild beasts" with the children, and frighten them into fits that would last all night.

So far as intention went, he was the kindest man alive. He never visited poor sick persons without taking with him in his pocket some little delicacy calculated to disagree with them and make them worse. He arranged yachting excursions for bad sailors, entirely at his own expense, and seemed to regard their subsequent agonies as ingratitude.

He loved to manage a wedding. Once he planned matters so that the bride arrived at the altar three-quarters of an hour before the groom, which led to unpleasantness upon a day that should have been filled only with joy, and once he forgot the clergyman. But he was always ready to admit when he made a mistake.

At funerals, also, he was to the fore, pointing out to the grief-stricken relatives how much better it was for all concerned that the corpse was dead, and expressing a pious hope that they would soon join it.

The chiefest delight of his life, however, was to be mixed up in other people's domestic quarrels. No domestic quarrel for miles round was complete without him. He generally came in as mediator, and finished as leading witness for the appellant.

As a journalist or politician his wonderful grasp of other people's business would have won for him esteem. The error he made was working it out in practice.

THE MAN WHO
LIVED FOR OTHERS

The first time we met, to speak, he was sitting with his back against a pollard willow, smoking a clay pipe. He smoked it very slowly, but very conscientiously. After each whiff he removed the pipe from his mouth and fanned away the smoke with his cap.

"Feeling bad?" I asked from behind a tree, at the same time making ready for a run, big boys' answers to small boys' impertinences being usually of the nature of things best avoided.

To my surprise and relief — for at second glance I perceived I had under-estimated the length of his legs — he appeared to regard the question as a natural and proper one, replying with unaffected candour, "Not yet."

My desire became to comfort him — a sentiment I think he understood and was grateful for. Advancing into the open, I sat down over against him, and watched him for a while in silence. Presently he said: —

"Have you ever tried drinking beer?"

I admitted I had not.

"Oh, it is beastly stuff," he rejoined with an involuntary shudder.

Rendered forgetful of present trouble by bitter recollection of the past, he puffed away at his pipe carelessly and without judgment.

"Do you often drink it?" I inquired.

"Yes," he replied gloomily; "all we fellows in the fifth form drink beer and smoke pipes."

A deeper tinge of green spread itself over his face.

He rose suddenly and made towards the hedge. Before he reached it, however, he stopped and addressed me, but without turning round.

"If you follow me, young 'un, or look, I'll punch your head," he said swiftly, and disappeared with a gurgle.

He left at the end of the terms and I did not see him again until we were both young men. Then one day I ran against him in Oxford Street, and he asked me to come and spend a few days with his people in Surrey.

I found him wan-looking and depressed, and every now and then he sighed. During a walk across the common he cheered up considerably, but the moment we got back to the house door he seemed to recollect himself, and began to sigh again. He ate no dinner whatever, merely sipping a glass of wine and crumbling a piece of bread. I was troubled at noticing this, but his relatives — a maiden aunt, who kept house, two elder sisters, and a weak-eyed female cousin who had left her husband behind her in India — were evidently charmed. They glanced at each other, and nodded and smiled. Once in a fit of abstraction he swallowed a bit of crust, and immediately they all looked pained and surprised.

In the drawing-room, under cover of a sentimental song, sung by the female cousin, I questioned his aunt on the subject.

"What's the matter with him?" I said. "Is he ill?"

The old lady chuckled.

"You'll be like that one day," she whispered gleefully.

"When," I asked, not unnaturally alarmed.

"When you're in love," she answered.

"Is *he* in love?" I inquired after a pause.

"Can't you see he is?" she replied somewhat scornfully.

I was a young man, and interested in the question.

"Won't he ever eat any dinner till he's got over it?" I asked.

She looked round sharply at me, but apparently decided that I was only foolish.

"You wait till your time comes," she answered, shaking her curls at me. "You won't care much about your dinner — not if you are *really* in love."

In the night, about half-past eleven, I heard, as I thought, foot-steps in the passage, and creeping to the door and opening it I saw the figure of my friend in dressing-gown and slippers, vanishing down the stairs. My idea was that, his brain weakened by trouble, he had developed sleep-walking tendencies. Partly out of curiosity, partly to watch over him, I slipped on a pair of trousers and fol-lowed him.

He placed his candle on the kitchen table and made a bee-line for the pantry door, from where he subsequently emerged with two pounds of cold beef on a plate and about a quart of beer in a jug; and I came away, leaving him fumbling for pickles.

I assisted at his wedding, where it seemed to me he endeavoured to display more ecstasy than it was possible for any human being to feel; and fifteen months later, happening to catch sight of an advertisement in the births column of *The Times*, I called on my way home from the City to congratulate him. He was pacing up and down the passage with his hat on, pausing at intervals to partake of an uninviting-looking meal, consisting of a cold mutton chop and a glass of lemonade, spread out upon a chair. Seeing that the cook and the housemaid were wandering about the house evidently bored for want of something to do, and that the dining-room, where he would have been much more out of the way, was empty and quite in order, I failed at first to understand the reason for his deliberate choice of discomfort. I, however, kept my reflections to myself, and inquired after the mother and child.

"Couldn't be better," he replied with a groan. "The doctor said he'd never had a more satisfactory case in all his experience."

"Oh, I'm glad to hear that," I answered; "I was afraid you'd been worrying yourself."

"Worried!" he exclaimed. "My dear boy, I don't know whether I'm standing on my head or my heels" (he gave one that idea). "This is the first morsel of food that's passed my lips for twenty-four hours."

At this moment the nurse appeared at the top of the stairs. He flew towards her, upsetting the lemonade in his excitement.

"What is it?" he asked hoarsely. "Is it all right?"

The old lady glanced from him to his cold chop, and smiled approvingly.

"They're doing splendidly," she answered, patting him on the shoulder in a motherly fashion. "Don't you worry."

"I can't help it, Mrs. Jobson," he replied, sitting down upon the bottom stair, and leaning his head against the banisters.

"Of course you can't," said Mrs. Jobson admiringly; "and you wouldn't be much of a man if you could." Then it was borne in upon me why he wore his hat, and dined off cold chops in the passage.

The following summer they rented a picturesque old house in Berkshire, and invited me down from a Saturday to Monday. Their place was near the river, so I slipped a suit of flannels in my bag, and on the Sunday morning I came down in them. He met me in the garden. He was dressed in a frock coat and a white waistcoat; and I noticed that he kept looking at me out of the corner of his eye, and that he seemed to have a trouble on his mind. The first breakfast bell rang, and then he said, "You haven't got any proper clothes with you, have you?"

"Proper clothes!" I exclaimed, stopping in some alarm. "Why, has anything given way?"

"No, not that," he explained. "I mean clothes to go to church in."

"Church," I said. "You're surely not going to church a fine day like this? I made sure you'd be playing tennis, or going on the river. You always used to."

"Yes," he replied, nervously flicking a rose-bush with a twig he had picked up. "You see, it isn't ourselves exactly. Maud and I would rather like to, but our cook, she's Scotch, and a little strict in her notions."

"And does she insist on your going to church every Sunday morning?" I inquired.

"Well," he answered, "she thinks it strange if we don't, and so we generally do, just in the morning — and evening. And then in the afternoon a few of the village girls drop in, and we have a little singing and that sort of thing. I never like hurting anyone's feelings if I can help it."

I did not say what I thought. Instead I said, "I've got that tweed suit I wore yesterday. I can put that on if you like."

He ceased flicking the rose-bush, and knitted his brows. He seemed to be recalling it to his imagination.

"No," he said, shaking his head, "I'm afraid it would shock her. It's my fault, I know," he added, remorsefully. "I ought to have told you."

Then an idea came to him.

"I suppose," he said, "you wouldn't care to pretend you were ill, and stop in bed just for the day?"

I explained that my conscience would not permit my being a party to such deception

"No, I thought you wouldn't," he replied. "I must explain it to her. I think I'll say you've lost your bag. I shouldn't like her to think bad of us."

Later on a fourteenth cousin died, leaving him a large fortune. He purchased an estate in Yorkshire, and became a "county family," and then his real troubles began.

From May to the middle of August, save for a little fly fishing, which generally resulted in his getting his feet wet and catching a cold, life was fairly peaceful; but from early autumn to late spring he found the work decidedly trying. He was a stout man, constitutionally nervous of fire-arms, and a six-hours' tramp with a heavy gun across ploughed fields, in company with a crowd of careless persons who kept blazing away within an inch of other people's noses, harassed and exhausted him. He had to get out of bed at four on chilly October mornings to go cub-hunting, and twice a week throughout the winter — except when a blessed frost brought him a brief respite — he had to ride to hounds. That he usually got off with nothing more serious than mere bruises and slight concussions of the spine, he probably owed to the fortunate circumstances of his being little and fat. At stiff timber he shut his eyes and rode hard; and ten yards from a river he would begin to think about bridges.

Yet he never complained.

"If you are a country gentleman," he would say, "you must behave as a country gentleman, and take the rough with the smooth."

As ill fate would have it a chance speculation doubled his fortune, and it became necessary that he should go into Parliament and start a yacht. Parliament made his head ache, and the yacht made him sick. Notwithstanding, every summer he would fill it with a lot of expensive people who bored him, and sail away for a month's misery in the Mediterranean.

During one cruise his guests built up a highly-interesting gambling scandal. He himself was confined to his cabin at the time, and knew nothing about it; but the Opposition papers, getting hold of the story, referred casually to the yacht as a "floating hell," and *The Police News* awarded his portrait the place of honour as the chief criminal of the week.

Later on he got into a cultured set, ruled by a thick-lipped undergraduate. His favourite literature had hitherto been of the Corelli and *Tit-Bits* order, but now he read Meredith and the yellow book, and tried to understand them; and instead of the Gaiety, he subscribed to the Independent Theatre, and fed "his soul," on Dutch Shakespeares. What he liked in art was a pretty girl by a cottage-door with an eligible young man in the background, or a child and a dog doing something funny. They told him these things were wrong and made him buy "Impressions" that stirred his liver to its deepest depths every time he looked at them — green cows on red hills by pink moonlight, or scarlet-haired corpses with three feet of neck.

He said meekly that such seemed to him unnatural, but they answered that nature had nothing to do with the question; that the artist saw things like that, and that whatever an artist saw — no matter in what condition he may have been when he saw it — that was art.

They took him to Wagner festivals and Burne-Jones's private views. They read him all the minor poets. They booked seats for him at all Ibsen's plays. They introduced him into all the most soulful circles of artistic society. His days were one long feast of other people's enjoyments.

One morning I met him coming down the steps of the Arts Club. He looked weary. He was just off to a private view at the New Gallery. In the afternoon he had to attend an amateur performance of "The Cenci," given by the Shelley Society. Then followed three literary and artistic At Homes, a dinner with an Indian nabob who couldn't speak a word of English, "Tristam and Isolde" at Covent Garden Theatre, and a ball at Lord Salisbury's to wind up the day.

I laid my hand upon his shoulder.

"Come with me to Epping Forest," I said. "There's a four-horse brake starts from Charing Cross at eleven. It's Saturday, and there's bound to be a crowd down there. I'll play you a game of skittles, and we will have a shy at the cocoa-nuts. You used to be rather smart at cocoa-nuts. We can have lunch there and be back at seven, dine at the Troc., spend the evening at the Empire, and sup at the Savoy. What do you say?"

He stood hesitating on the steps, a wistful look in his eyes.

His brougham drew up against the curb, and he started as if from a dream.

"My dear fellow," he replied, "what would people say?" And shaking me by the hand, he took his seat, and the footman slammed the door upon him.

A MAN OF HABIT

There were three of us in the smoke-room of the *Alexandra* — a very good friend of mine, myself, and, in the opposite corner, a shy-looking, unobtrusive man, the editor, as we subsequently learned, of a New York Sunday paper.

My friend and I were discussing habits, good and bad.

"After the first few months," said my friend, "it is no more effort for a man to be a saint than to be a sinner; it becomes a mere matter of habit."

"I know," I interrupted, "it is every whit as easy to spring out of bed the instant you are called as to say 'All Right,' and turn over for just another five minutes' snooze, when you have got into the way of it. It is no more trouble not to swear than to swear, if you make a custom of it. Toast and water is as delicious as champagne, when you have acquired the taste for it. Things are also just as easy the other way about. It is a mere question of making your choice and sticking to it."

He agreed with me.

"Now take these cigars of mine," he said, pushing his open case towards me.

"Thank you," I replied hurriedly, "I'm not smoking this passage."

"Don't be alarmed," he answered, "I meant merely as an argument. Now one of these would make you wretched for a week."

I admitted his premise.

"Very well," he continued. "Now I, as you know, smoke them all day long, and enjoy them. Why? Because I have got into the habit. Years ago, when I was a young man, I smoked expensive Havanas. I found that I was ruining myself. It was absolutely necessary that I should take a cheaper weed. I was living in Belgium at the time, and a friend showed me these. I don't know what they are — probably cabbage leaves soaked in guano; they tasted to me like that at first — but they were cheap. Buying them by the five hundred, they cost me three a penny. I determined to like them, and started with one a day. It was terrible work, I admit, but as I said to myself, nothing could be worse than the Havanas themselves had been in the beginning. Smoking is an acquired taste, and it must be as easy to learn to like one flavour as another. I persevered and I conquered. Before the year was over I could think of them without loathing, at the end of two I could smoke them without positive discomfort. Now I prefer them to any other brand on the market. Indeed, a good cigar disagrees with me."

I suggested it might have been less painful to have given up smoking altogether.

"I did think of it," he replied, "but a man who doesn't smoke always seems to me bad company. There is something very sociable about smoke."

He leant back and puffed great clouds into the air, filling the small den with an odour suggestive of bilge water and cemeteries.

"Then again," he resumed after a pause, "take my claret. No, you don't like it." (I had not spoken, but my face had evidently betrayed me.) "Nobody does, at least no one I have ever met. Three years ago, when I was living in Hammersmith, we caught two burglars with it. They broke open the sideboard, and swallowed five bottlefuls between them. A policeman found them afterwards, sitting on a doorstep a hundred yards off, the 'swag' beside them in a carpet bag. They were too ill to offer any resistance, and went to the station like lambs, he promising to send the doctor to them the moment they were safe in the cells. Ever since then I have left out a decanterful upon the table every night.

"Well, I like that claret, and it does me good. I come in sometimes dead beat. I drink a couple of glasses, and I'm a new man. I took to it in the first instance for the same reason that I took to the cigars — it was cheap. I have it sent over direct from Geneva, and it costs me six shillings a dozen. How they do it I don't know. I don't want to know. As you may remember, it's fairly heady and there's body in it.

"I knew one man," he continued, "who had a regular Mrs. Caudle of a wife. All day long she talked to him, or at him, or of him, and at night he fell asleep to the rising and falling rhythm of what she thought about him. At last she died, and his friends congratulated him, telling him that now he would enjoy peace. But it was the peace of the desert, and the man did not enjoy it. For two-and-twenty years her voice had filled the house, penetrated through the conservatory, and floated in faint shrilly waves of sound round the garden, and out into the road beyond. The silence now pervading everywhere frightened and disturbed him. The place was no longer home to him. He missed the breezy morning insult, the long winter evening's reproaches beside the flickering fire. At night he could not sleep. For hours he would lie tossing restlessly, his ears aching for the accustomed soothing flow of invective.

"'Ah!' he would cry bitterly to himself, 'it is the old story, we never know the value of a thing until we have lost it.'

"He grew ill. The doctors dosed him with sleeping draughts in vain. At last they told him bluntly that his life depended upon his finding another wife, able and willing to nag him to sleep.

"There were plenty of wives of the type he wanted in the neighbourhood, but the unmarried women were, of necessity, inexperienced, and his health was such that he could not afford the time to train them.

"Fortunately, just as despair was about to take possession of him, a man died in the next parish, literally talked to death, the gossip said, by his wife. He obtained an introduction, and called upon her the day after the funeral. She was a cantankerous old woman, and the wooing was a harassing affair, but his heart was in his work, and before six months were gone he had won her for his own.

"She proved, however, but a poor substitute. The spirit was willing but the flesh was weak. She had neither that command of language nor of wind that had distinguished her rival. From his favourite seat at the bottom of the garden he could not hear her at all, so he had his chair brought up into the conservatory. It was all right for him there so long she continued to abuse him; but every now and again, just as he was getting comfortably settled down with his pipe and his newspaper, she would suddenly stop.

"He would drop his paper and sit listening, with a troubled, anxious expression.

"'Are you there, dear?' he would call out after a while.

"'Yes, I'm here. Where do you think I am you old fool?' she would gasp back in an exhausted voice.

"His face would brighten at the sound of her words. 'Go on, dear,' he would answer. 'I'm listening. I like to hear you talk.'

"But the poor woman was utterly pumped out, and had not so much as a snort left.

"Then he would shake his head sadly. 'No, she hasn't poor dear Susan's flow,' he would say. 'Ah! what a woman that was!'

"At night she would do her best, but it was a lame and halting performance by comparison. After rating him for little over three-quarters of an hour, she would sink back on the pillow, and want to go to sleep. But he would shake her gently by the shoulder.

"'Yes, dear,' he would say, 'you were speaking about Jane, and the way I kept looking at her during lunch.'

"It's extraordinary," concluded my friend, lighting a fresh cigar, "what creatures of habit we are."

"Very," I replied. "I knew a man who told tall stories till when he told a true one nobody believed it."

"Ah, that was a very sad case," said my friend.

"Speaking of habit," said the unobtrusive man in the corner, "I can tell you a true story that I'll bet my bottom dollar you won't believe."

"Haven't got a bottom dollar, but I'll bet you half a sovereign I do," replied my friend, who was of a sporting turn. "Who shall be judge?"

"I'll take your word for it," said the unobtrusive man, and started straight away.

"He was a Jefferson man, this man I'm going to tell you of," he begun. "He was born in the town, and for forty-seven years he never slept a night outside it. He was a most respectable man — a drysalter from nine to four, and a Presbyterian in his leisure moments. He said that a good life merely meant good habits. He rose at seven, had family prayer at seven-thirty, breakfasted at eight, got to his business at nine, had his horse brought round to the office at four, and rode for an hour, reached home at five, had a bath and a cup of tea, played with and read to the children (he was a domesticated man) till half-past six, dressed and dined at seven, went round to the club and played whist till quarter after ten, home again to evening prayer at ten-thirty, and bed at eleven. For five-and-twenty years he lived that life with never a variation. It worked into his system and became mechanical. The church clocks were set by him. He was used by the local astronomers to check the sun.

"One day a distant connection of his in London, an East Indian Merchant and an ex-Lord Mayor died, leaving him sole legatee and executor. The business was a complicated one and needed management. He determined to leave his son by his first wife, now a young man of twenty-four, in charge at Jefferson, and to establish himself with his second family in England, and look after the East Indian business.

"He set out from Jefferson City on October the fourth, and arrived in London on the seventeenth. He had been ill during the whole of the voyage, and he reached the furnished house he had hired in Bayswater somewhat of a wreck. A couple of days in bed, however, pulled him round, and on the Wednesday evening he announced his intention of going into the City the next day to see to his affairs.

"On the Thursday morning he awoke at one o'clock. His wife told him she had not disturbed him, thinking the sleep would do him good. He admitted that perhaps it had. Anyhow, he felt very well, and he got up and dressed himself. He said he did not like the idea of beginning his first day by neglecting a religious duty, and his wife agreeing with him, they assembled the servants and the children in the dining-room, and had family prayer at half-past one. After which he breakfasted and set off, reaching the City about three.

"His reputation for punctuality had preceded him, and surprise was everywhere expressed at his late arrival. He explained the circumstances, however, and made his appointments for the following day to commence from nine-thirty.

"He remained at the office until late, and then went home. For dinner, usually the chief meal of the day, he could manage to eat only a biscuit and some fruit. He attributed his loss of appetite to want of his customary ride. He was strangely unsettled all the evening. He said he supposed he missed his game of whist, and determined to look about him without loss of time for some quiet, respectable club. At eleven he retired with his wife to bed, but could not sleep. He tossed and turned, and turned and tossed, but grew only more and more wakeful and energetic. A little after midnight an overpowering desire seized him to go and wish the children good-night. He slipped on a dressing-gown and stole into the nursery. He did not intend it, but the opening of the door awoke them, and he was glad. He wrapped them up in the quilt, and, sitting on the edge of the bed, told them moral stories till one o'clock.

"Then he kissed them, bidding them be good and go to sleep; and finding himself painfully hungry, crept downstairs, where in the back kitchen he made a hearty meal off cold game pie and cucumber.

"He retired to bed feeling more peaceful, yet still could not sleep, so lay thinking about his business affairs till five, when he dropped off.

"At one o'clock to the minute he awoke. His wife told him she had made every endeavour to rouse him, but in vain. The man was vexed and irritated. If he had not been a very good man indeed, I believe he would have sworn. The same programme was repeated as on the Thursday, and again he reached the City at three.

"This state of things went on for a month. The man fought against himself, but was unable to alter himself. Every morning, or rather every afternoon at one he awoke. Every night at one he crept down into the kitchen and foraged for food. Every morning at five he fell asleep.

"He could not understand it, nobody could understand it. The doctor treated him for water on the brain, hypnotic irresponsibility and hereditary lunacy. Meanwhile his business suffered, and his health grew worse. He seemed to be living upside down. His days seemed to have neither beginning nor end, but to be all middle. There was no time for exercise or recreation. When he began to feel cheerful and sociable everybody else was asleep.

"One day by chance the explanation came. His eldest daughter was preparing her home studies after dinner.

"'What time is it now in New York?' she asked, looking up from her geography book.

"'New York,' said her father, glancing at his watch, 'let me see. It's just ten now, and there's a little over four and a half hours' difference. Oh, about half-past five in the afternoon.'

"'Then in Jefferson,' said the mother, 'it would be still earlier, wouldn't it?'

"'Yes,' replied the girl, examining the map, 'Jefferson is nearly two degrees further west.'

"'Two degrees,' mused the father, 'and there's forty minutes to a degree. That would make it now, at the present moment in Jefferson — '

He leaped to his feet with a cry:

"'I've got it!' he shouted, 'I see it.'

"'See what?' asked his wife, alarmed.

"'Why, it's four o'clock in Jefferson, and just time for my ride. That's what I'm wanting.'

"There could be no doubt about it. For five-and-twenty years he had lived by clockwork. But it was by Jefferson clockwork, not London clockwork. He had changed his longitude, but not himself. The habits of a quarter of a century were not to be shifted at the bidding of the sun.

"He examined the problem in all its bearings, and decided that the only solution was for him to return to the order of his old life. He saw the difficulties in his way, but they were less than those he was at present encountering. He was too formed by habit to adapt himself to circumstances. Circumstances must adapt themselves to him.

"He fixed his office hours from three till ten, leaving himself at half-past nine. At ten he mounted his horse and went for a canter in the Row, and on very dark nights he carried a lantern. News of it got abroad, and crowds would assemble to see him ride past.

"He dined at one o'clock in the morning, and afterwards strolled down to his club. He had tried to discover a quiet, respectable club where the members were willing to play whist till four in the morning, but failing, had been compelled to join a small Soho gambling-hell, where they taught him poker. The place was occasionally raided by the police, but thanks to his respectable appearance, he generally managed to escape.

"At half-past four he returned home, and woke up the family for evening prayers. At five he went to bed and slept like a top.

"The City chaffed him, and Bayswater shook its head over him, but that he did not mind. The only thing that really troubled him was loss of spiritual communion. At five o'clock on Sunday afternoons he felt he wanted chapel, but had to do without it. At seven he ate his simple mid-day meal. At eleven he had tea and muffins, and at midnight he began to crave again for hymns and sermons. At three he had a bread-and-cheese supper, and retired early at four a.m., feeling sad and unsatisfied.

"He was essentially a man of habit."

The unobtrusive stranger ceased, and we sat gazing in silence at the ceiling.

At length my friend rose, and taking half-a-sovereign from his pocket, laid it upon the table, and linking his arm in mine went out with me upon the deck.

THE ABSENT-MINDED MAN

You ask him to dine with you on Thursday to meet a few people who are anxious to know him.

"Now don't make a muddle of it," you say, recollectful of former mishaps, "and come on the Wednesday."

He laughs good-naturedly as he hunts through the room for his diary.

"Shan't be able to come Wednesday," he says, "shall be at the Mansion House, sketching dresses, and on Friday I start for Scotland, so as to be at the opening of the Exhibition on Saturday. It's bound to be all right this time. Where the deuce is that diary! Never mind, I'll make a note of it on this — you can see me do it."

You stand over him while he writes the appointment down on a sheet of foolscap, and watch him pin it up over his desk. Then you come away contented.

"I do hope he'll turn up," you say to your wife on the Thursday evening, while dressing.

"Are you sure you made it clear to him?" she replies, suspiciously, and you instinctively feel that whatever happens she is going to blame you for it.

Eight o'clock arrives, and with it the other guests. At half-past eight your wife is beckoned mysteriously out of the room, where the parlour-maid informs her that the cook has expressed a determination, in case of further delay, to wash her hands, figuratively speaking, of the whole affair.

Your wife, returning, suggests that if the dinner is to be eaten at all it had better be begun. She evidently considers that in pretending to expect him you have been merely playing a part, and that it would have been manlier and more straightforward for you to have admitted at the beginning that you had forgotten to invite him.

During the soup and the fish you recount anecdotes of his unpunctuality. By the time the *entrée* arrives the empty chair has begun to cast a gloom over the dinner, and with the joint the conversation drifts into talk about dead relatives.

On Friday, at a quarter past eight, he dashes to the door and rings violently. Hearing his voice in the hall, you go to meet him.

"Sorry I'm late," he sings out cheerily. "Fool of a cabman took me to Alfred Place instead of —"

"Well, what do you want now you are come?" you interrupt, feeling anything but genially inclined towards him. He is an old friend, so you can be rude to him.

He laughs, and slaps you on the shoulder.

"Why, my dinner, my dear boy, I'm starving."

"Oh," you grunt in reply. "Well, you go and get it somewhere else, then. You're not going to have it here."

"What the devil do you mean?" he says. "You asked me to dinner."

"I did nothing of the kind," you tell him. "I asked you to dinner on Thursday, not on Friday."

He stares at you incredulously.

"How did I get Friday fixed in my mind?" inquiringly.

"Because yours is the sort of mind that would get Friday firmly fixed into it, when Thursday was the day," you explain. "I thought you had to be off to Edinburgh to-night," you add.

"Great Scott!" he cries, "so I have."

And without another word he dashes out, and you hear him rushing down the road, shouting for the cab he has just dismissed.

As you return to your study you reflect that he will have to travel all the way to Scotland in evening dress, and will have to send out the hotel porter in the morning to buy him a suit of ready-made clothes, and are glad.

Matters work out still more awkwardly when it is he who is the host. I remember being with him on his house-boat one day. It was a little after twelve, and we were sitting on the edge of the boat, dangling our feet in the river — the spot was a lonely one, half-way between Wallingford and Day's Lock. Suddenly round the bend appeared two skiffs, each one containing six elaborately-dressed persons. As soon as they caught sight of us they began waving handkerchiefs and parasols.

"Hullo!" I said, "here's some people hailing you."

"Oh, they all do that about here," he answered, without looking up. "Some beanfeast from Abingdon, I expect."

The boats draw nearer. When about two hundred yards off an elderly gentleman raised himself up in the prow of the leading one and shouted to us.

McQuae heard his voice, and gave a start that all but pitched him into the water.

"Good God!" he cried, "I'd forgotten all about it."

"About what?" I asked.

"Why, it's the Palmers and the Grahams and the Hendersons. I've asked them all over to lunch, and there's not a blessed thing on board but two mutton chops and a pound of potatoes, and I've given the boy a holiday."

Another day I was lunching with him at the Junior Hogarth,

when a man named Hallyard, a mutual friend, strolled across to us.

"What are you fellows going to do this afternoon?" he asked, seating himself the opposite side of the table.

"I'm going to stop here and write letters," I answered.

"Come with me if you want something to do," said McQuae. "I'm going to drive Leena down to Richmond." ("Leena" was the young lady he recollected being engaged to. It transpired afterwards that he was engaged to three girls at the time. The other two he had forgotten all about.) "It's a roomy seat at the back."

"Oh, all right," said Hallyard, and they went away together in a hansom.

An hour and a half later Hallyard walked into the smoking-room looking depressed and worn, and flung himself into a chair.

"I thought you were going to Richmond with McQuae," I said.

"So did I," he answered.

"Had an accident?" I asked.

"Yes."

He was decidedly curt in his replies.

"Cart upset?" I continued.

"No, only me."

His grammar and his nerves seemed thoroughly shaken.

I waited for an explanation, and after a while he gave it.

"We got to Putney," he said, "with just an occasional run into a tram-car, and were going up the hill, when suddenly he turned a corner. You know his style at a corner — over the curb, across the road, and into the opposite lamp-post. Of course, as a rule one is prepared for it, but I never reckoned on his turning up there, and the first thing I recollect is finding myself sitting in the middle of the street with a dozen fools grinning at me.

"It takes a man a few minutes in such a case to think where he is and what has happened, and when I got up they were some distance away. I ran after them for a quarter of a mile, shouting at the top of my voice, and accompanied by a mob of boys, all yelling like hell on a Bank Holiday. But one might as well have tried to hail the dead, so I took the 'bus back.

"They might have guessed what had happened," he added, "by the shifting of the cart, if they'd had any sense. I'm not a light-weight."

He complained of soreness, and said he would go home. I suggested a cab, but he replied that he would rather walk.

I met McQuae in the evening at the St. James's Theatre. It was a first night, and he was taking sketches for *The Graphic*. The moment he saw me he made his way across to me.

"The very man I wanted to see," he said. "Did I take Hallyard with me in the cart to Richmond this afternoon?"

"You did," I replied.

"So Leena says," he answered, greatly bewildered, "but I'll swear he wasn't there when we got to the Queen's Hotel."

"It's all right," I said, "you dropped him at Putney."

"Dropped him at Putney!" he repeated. "I've no recollection of doing so."

"He has," I answered. "You ask him about it. He's full of it."

Everybody said he never would get married; that it was absurd to suppose he ever would remember the day, the church, and the girl, all in one morning; that if he did get as far as the altar he would forget what he had come for, and would give the bride away to his own best man. Hallyard had an idea that he was already married, but that the fact had slipped his memory. I myself felt sure that if he did marry he would forget all about it the next day.

But everybody was wrong. By some miraculous means the ceremony got itself accomplished, so that if Hallyard's idea be correct (as to which there is every possibility), there will be trouble. As for my own fears, I dismissed them the moment I saw the lady. She was a charming, cheerful little woman, but did not look the type that would let him forget all about it.

I had not seen him since his marriage, which had happened in the spring. Working my way back from Scotland by easy stages, I stopped for a few days at Scarboro'. After *table d'hôte* I put on my mackintosh, and went out for a walk. It was raining hard, but after a month in Scotland one does not notice English weather, and I wanted some air. Struggling along the dark beach with my head against the wind, I stumbled over a crouching figure, seeking to shelter itself a little from the storm under the lee of the Spa wall.

I expected it to swear at me, but it seemed too broken-spirited to mind anything.

"I beg your pardon," I said. "I did not see you."

At the sound of my voice it started to its feet.

"Is that you, old man?" it cried.

"McQuae!" I exclaimed.

"By Jove!" he said, "I was never so glad to see a man in all my life before."

And he nearly shook my hand off.

"But what in thunder!" I said, "are you doing here? Why, you're drenched to the skin."

He was dressed in flannels and a tennis-coat.

"Yes," he answered. "I never thought it would rain. It was a lovely morning."

I began to fear he had overworked himself into a brain fever.

"Why don't you go home?" I asked.

"I can't," he replied. "I don't know where I live. I've forgotten the address."

"For heaven's sake," he said, "take me somewhere, and give me something to eat. I'm literally starving."

"Haven't you any money?" I asked him, as we turned towards the hotel.

"Not a sou," he answered. "We got in here from York, the wife and I, about eleven. We left our things at the station, and started to hunt for apartments. As soon as we were fixed, I changed my clothes and came out for a walk, telling Maud I should be back at one to lunch. Like a fool, I never took the address, and never noticed the way I was going.

"It's an awful business," he continued. "I don't see how I'm ever going to find her. I hoped she might stroll down to the Spa in the evening, and I've been hanging about the gates ever since six. I hadn't the threepence to go in."

"But have you no notion of the sort of street or the kind of house it was?" I enquired.

"Not a ghost," he replied. "I left it all to Maud, and didn't trouble."

"Have you tried any of the lodging-houses?" I asked.

"Tried!" he exclaimed bitterly. "I've been knocking at doors, and asking if Mrs. McQuae lives there steadily all the afternoon, and they slam the door in my face, mostly without answering. I told a policeman — I thought perhaps he might suggest something — but the idiot only burst out laughing, and that made me so mad that I gave him a black eye, and had to cut. I expect they're on the lookout for me now."

"I went into a restaurant," he continued gloomily, "and tried to get them to trust me for a steak. But the proprietress said she'd heard that tale before, and ordered me out before all the other customers. I think I'd have drowned myself if you hadn't turned up."

After a change of clothes and some supper, he discussed the case more calmly, but it was really a serious affair. They had shut up their flat, and his wife's relatives were travelling abroad. There was no one to whom he could send a letter to be forwarded; there was no one with whom she would be likely to communicate. Their chance of meeting again in this world appeared remote.

Nor did it seem to me — fond as he was of his wife, and anxious as he undoubtedly was to recover her — that he looked forward to the actual meeting, should it ever arrive, with any too pleasurable anticipation.

"She will think it strange," he murmured reflectively, sitting on the edge of the bed, and thoughtfully pulling off his socks. "She is sure to think it strange."

The following day, which was Wednesday, we went to a solicitor, and laid the case before him, and he instituted inquiries among all the lodging-house keepers in Scarborough, with the result that on Thursday afternoon McQuae was restored (after the manner of an Adelphi hero in the last act) to his home and wife.

I asked him next time I met him what she had said.

"Oh, much what I expected," he replied.

But he never told me what he had expected.

A CHARMING WOMAN

"Not *the Mr. —-, really?*"

In her deep brown eyes there lurked pleased surprise, struggling with wonder. She looked from myself to the friend who introduced us with a bewitching smile of incredulity, tempered by hope.

He assured her, adding laughingly, "The only genuine and original," and left us.

"I've always thought of you as a staid, middle-aged man," she said, with a delicious little laugh, then added in low soft tones, "I'm so very pleased to meet you, really."

The words were conventional, but her voice crept round one like a warm caress.

"Come and talk to me," she said, seating herself upon a small settee, and making room for me.

I sat down awkwardly beside her, my head buzzing just a little, as with one glass too many of champagne. I was in my literary childhood. One small book and a few essays and criticisms, scattered through various obscure periodicals had been as yet my only contributions to current literature. The sudden discovery that I was the Mr. Anybody, and that charming women thought of me, and were delighted to meet me, was a brain-disturbing thought.

"And it was really you who wrote that clever book?" she continued, "and all those brilliant things, in the magazines and journals. Oh, it must be delightful to be clever."

She gave breath to a little sigh of vain regret that went to my heart. To console her I commenced a laboured compliment, but she stopped me with her fan. On after reflection I was glad she had — it would have been one of those things better expressed otherwise.

"I know what you are going to say," she laughed, "but don't. Besides, from you I should not know quite how to take it. You can be so satirical."

I tried to look as though I could be, but in her case would not.

She let her ungloved hand rest for an instant upon mine. Had she left it there for two, I should have gone down on my knees before her, or have stood on my head at her feet — have made a fool of myself in some way or another before the whole room full. She timed it to a nicety.

"I don't want *you* to pay me compliments," she said, "I want us to be friends. Of course, in years, I'm old enough to be your mother." (By the register I should say she might have been thirty-two, but looked twenty-six. I was twenty-three, and I fear foolish for my age.) "But you know the world, and you're so different to the other people one meets. Society is so hollow and artificial; don't you find it so? You don't know how I long sometimes to get away from it, to know someone to whom I could show my real self, who would understand me. You'll come and see me sometimes — I'm always at home on Wednesdays — and let me talk to you, won't you, and you must tell me all your clever thoughts."

It occurred to me that, maybe, she would like to hear a few of them there and then, but before I had got well started a hollow Society man came up and suggested supper, and she was compelled to leave me. As she disappeared, however, in the throng, she looked back over her shoulder with a glance half pathetic, half comic, that I understood. It said, "Pity me, I've got to be bored by this vapid, shallow creature," and I did.

I sought her through all the rooms before I went. I wished to assure her of my sympathy and support. I learned, however, from the butler that she had left early, in company with the hollow Society man.

A fortnight later I ran against a young literary friend in Regent Street, and we lunched together at the Monico.

"I met such a charming woman last night," he said, "a Mrs. Clifton Courtenay, a delightful woman."

"Oh, do *you* know her?" I exclaimed. "Oh, we're very old friends. She's always wanting me to go and see her. I really must."

"Oh, I didn't know *you* knew her," he answered. Somehow, the fact of my knowing her seemed to lessen her importance in his eyes. But soon he recovered his enthusiasm for her.

"A wonderfully clever woman," he continued. "I'm afraid I disappointed her a little though." He said this, however, with a laugh that contradicted his words. "She would not believe I was *the* Mr. Smith. She imagined from my book that I was quite an old man."

I could see nothing in my friend's book myself to suggest that the author was, of necessity, anything over eighteen. The mistake appeared to me to display want of acumen, but it had evidently pleased him greatly.

"I felt quite sorry for her," he went on, "chained to that bloodless, artificial society in which she lives. 'You can't tell,' she said to me, 'how I long to meet someone to whom I could show my real self — who would understand me.' I'm going to see her on Wednesday."

I went with him. My conversation with her was not as confidential as I had anticipated, owing to there being some eighty other people present in a room intended for the accommodation of eight;

but after surging round for an hour in hot and aimless misery — as very young men at such gatherings do, knowing as a rule only the man who has brought them, and being unable to find him — I contrived to get a few words with her.

She greeted me with a smile, in the light of which I at once forgot my past discomfort, and let her fingers rest, with delicious pressure, for a moment upon mine.

"How good of you to keep your promise," she said. "These people have been tiring me so. Sit here, and tell me all you have been doing."

She listened for about ten seconds, and then interrupted me with —

"And that clever friend of yours that you came with. I met him at dear Lady Lennon's last week. Has *he* written anything?"

I explained to her that he had.

"Tell me about it?" she said. "I get so little time for reading, and then I only care to read the books that help me," and she gave me a grateful look more eloquent than words.

I described the work to her, and wishing to do my friend justice I even recited a few of the passages upon which, as I knew, he especially prided himself.

One sentence in particular seemed to lay hold of her. "A good woman's arms round a man's neck is a lifebelt thrown out to him from heaven."

"How beautiful!" she murmured. "Say it again."

I said it again, and she repeated it after me.

Then a noisy old lady swooped down upon her, and I drifted away into a corner, where I tried to look as if I were enjoying myself, and failed.

Later on, feeling it time to go, I sought my friend, and found him talking to her in a corner. I approached and waited. They were discussing the latest east-end murder. A drunken woman had been killed by her husband, a hard-working artizan, who had been maddened by the ruin of his home.

"Ah," she was saying, "what power a woman has to drag a man down or lift him up. I never read a case in which a woman is concerned without thinking of those beautiful lines of yours: 'A good woman's arms round a man's neck is a lifebelt thrown out to him from heaven.'"

Opinions differed concerning her religion and politics. Said the Low Church parson: "An earnest Christian woman, sir, of that unostentatious type that has always been the bulwark of our

Church. I am proud to know that woman, and I am proud to think that poor words of mine have been the humble instrument to wean that true woman's heart from the frivolities of fashion, and to fix her thoughts upon higher things. A good Churchwoman, sir, a good Churchwoman, in the best sense of the word."

Said the pale aristocratic-looking young Abbé to the Comtesse, the light of old-world enthusiasm shining from his deep-set eyes: "I have great hopes for our dear friend. She finds it hard to sever the ties of time and love. We are all weak, but her heart turns towards our mother Church as a child, though suckled among strangers, yearns after many years for the bosom that has borne it. We have spoken, and I, even I, may be the voice in the wilderness leading the lost sheep back to the fold."

Said Sir Harry Bennett, the great Theosophist lecturer, writing to a friend: "A singularly gifted woman, and a woman evidently thirsting for the truth. A woman capable of willing her own life. A woman not afraid of thought and reason, a lover of wisdom. I have talked much with her at one time or another, and I have found her grasp my meaning with a quickness of perception quite unusual in my experience; and the arguments I have let fall, I am convinced, have borne excellent fruit. I look forward to her becoming, at no very distant date, a valued member of our little band. Indeed, without betraying confidence, I may almost say I regard her conversion as an accomplished fact."

Colonel Maxim always spoke of her as "a fair pillar of the State."

"With the enemy in our midst," said the florid old soldier, "it behoves every true man — aye, and every true woman — to rally to the defence of the country; and all honour, say I, to noble ladies such as Mrs. Clifton Courtenay, who, laying aside their natural shrinking from publicity, come forward in such a crisis as the present to combat the forces of disorder and disloyalty now rampant in the land."

"But," some listener would suggest, "I gathered from young Jocelyn that Mrs. Clifton Courtenay held somewhat advanced views on social and political questions."

"Jocelyn," the Colonel would reply with scorn; "pah! There may have been a short space of time during which the fellow's long hair and windy rhetoric impressed her. But I flatter myself I've put *my* spoke in Mr. Jocelyn's wheel. Why, damme, sir, she's consented to stand for Grand Dame of the Bermondsey Branch of the Primrose League next year. What's Jocelyn to say to that, the scoundrel!"

What Jocelyn said was: —

"I know the woman is weak. But I do not blame her; I pity her.

When the time comes, as soon it will, when woman is no longer a puppet, dancing to the threads held by some brainless man — when a woman is not threatened with social ostracism for daring to follow her own conscience instead of that of her nearest male relative — then will be the time to judge her. It is not for me to betray the confidence reposed in me by a suffering woman, but you can tell that interesting old fossil, Colonel Maxim, that he and the other old women of the Bermondsey Branch of the Primrose League may elect Mrs. Clifton Courtenay for their President, and make the most of it; they have only got the outside of the woman. Her heart is beating time to the tramp of an onward-marching people; her soul's eyes are straining for the glory of a coming dawn."

But they all agreed she was a charming woman.

WHIBLEY'S SPIRIT

I never met it myself, but I knew Whibley very well indeed, so that I came to hear a goodish deal about it.

It appeared to be devoted to Whibley, and Whibley was extremely fond of it. Personally I am not interested in spirits, and no spirit has ever interested itself in me. But I have friends whom they patronise, and my mind is quite open on the subject. Of Whibley's Spirit I wish to speak with every possible respect. It was, I am willing to admit, as hard-working and conscientious a spirit as any one could wish to live with. The only thing I have to say against it is that it had no sense.

It came with a carved cabinet that Whibley had purchased in Wardour Street for old oak, but which, as a matter of fact, was chestnut wood, manufactured in Germany, and at first was harmless enough, saying nothing but "Yes!" or "No!" and that only when spoken to.

Whibley would amuse himself of an evening asking it questions, being careful to choose tolerably simple themes, such as, "Are you there?" (to which the Spirit would sometimes answer "Yes!" and sometimes "No!") "Can you hear me?" "Are you happy?" — and so on. The Spirit made the cabinet crack — three times for "Yes" and twice for "No." Now and then it would reply both "Yes!" and "No!" to the same question, which Whibley attributed to overscrupulousness. When nobody asked it anything it would talk to itself, repeating "Yes!" "No!" "No!" "Yes!" over and over again in an aimless, lonesome sort of a way that made you feel sorry for it.

After a while Whibley bought a table, and encouraged it to launch out into more active conversation. To please Whibley, I assisted at some of the earlier séances, but during my presence it invariably maintained a reticence bordering on positive dulness. I gathered from Whibley that it disliked me, thinking that I was unsympathetic. The complaint was unjust; I was not unsympathetic, at least not at the commencement. I came to hear it talk, and I wanted to hear it talk; I would have listened to it by the hour. What tired me was its slowness in starting, and its foolishness when it had started, in using long words that it did not know how to spell. I remember on one occasion, Whibley, Jobstock (Whibley's partner), and myself, sitting for two hours, trying to understand what the thing meant by "H-e-s-t-u-r-n-e-m-y-s-f-e-a-r." It used no stops whatever. It never so much as hinted where one sentence ended and another began. It never even told us when it came to a proper name.

Its idea of an evening's conversation was to plump down a hundred or so vowels and consonants in front of you and leave you to make whatever sense out of them you could.

We fancied at first it was talking about somebody named Hester (it had spelt Hester with a "u" before we allowed a margin for spelling), and we tried to work the sentence out on that basis, "Hester enemies fear," we thought it might be. Whibley had a niece named Hester, and we decided the warning had reference to her. But whether she was our enemy, and we were to fear her, or whether we had to fear her enemies (and, if so, who were they?), or whether it was our enemies who were to be frightened by Hester, or her enemies, or enemies generally, still remained doubtful. We asked the table if it meant the first suggestion, and it said "No." We asked what it did mean, and it said "Yes."

This answer annoyed me, but Whibley explained that the Spirit was angry with us for our stupidity (which seemed quaint). He informed us that it always said first "No," and then "Yes," when it was angry, and as it was his Spirit, and we were in his house, we kept our feelings to ourselves and started afresh.

This time we abandoned the "Hestur" theory altogether. Jobstock suggested "Haste" for the first word, and, thought the Spirit might have gone on phonetically.

"Haste! you are here, Miss Sfear!" was what he made of it.

Whibley asked him sarcastically if he'd kindly explain what that meant.

I think Jobstock was getting irritable. We had been sitting cramped up round a wretched little one-legged table all the evening, and this was almost the first bit of gossip we had got out of it. To further excuse him, it should also be explained that the gas had been put out by Whibley, and that the fire had gone out of its own accord. He replied that it was hard labour enough to find out what the thing said without having to make sense of it.

"It can't spell," he added, "and it's got a nasty, sulky temper. If it was my spirit I'd hire another spirit to kick it."

Whibley was one of the mildest little men I ever knew, but chaff or abuse of his Spirit roused the devil in him, and I feared we were going to have a scene. Fortunately, I was able to get his mind back to the consideration of "Hesturnemysfear" before anything worse happened than a few muttered remarks about the laughter of fools, and want of reverence for sacred subjects being the sign of a shallow mind.

We tried "He's stern," and "His turn," and the "fear of Hesturnemy," and tried to think who "Hesturnemy" might be.

Three times we went over the whole thing again from the beginning, which meant six hundred and six tiltings of the table, and then suddenly the explanation struck me — "Eastern Hemisphere."

Whibley had asked it for any information it might possess concerning his wife's uncle, from whom he had not heard for months, and that apparently was its idea of an address.

The fame of Whibley's Spirit became noised abroad, with the result that Whibley was able to command the willing service of more congenial assistants, and Jobstock and myself were dismissed. But we bore no malice.

Under these more favourable conditions the Spirit plucked up wonderfully, and talked everybody's head off. It could never have been a cheerful companion, however, for its conversation was chiefly confined to warnings and prognostications of evil. About once a fortnight Whibley would drop round on me, in a friendly way, to tell me that I was to beware of a man who lived in a street beginning with a "C," or to inform me that if I would go to a town on the coast where there were three churches I should meet someone who would do me an irreparable injury, and, that I did not rush off then and there in search of that town he regarded as flying in the face of Providence.

In its passion for poking its ghostly nose into other people's affairs it reminded me of my earthly friend Poppleton. Nothing pleased it better than being appealed to for aid and advice, and Whibley, who was a perfect slave to it, would hunt half over the parish for people in trouble and bring them to it.

It would direct ladies, eager for divorce court evidence, to go to the third house from the corner of the fifth street, past such and such a church or public-house (it never would give a plain, straightforward address), and ring the bottom bell but one twice. They would thank it effusively, and next morning would start to find the fifth street past the church, and would ring the bottom bell but one of the third house from the corner twice, and a man in his shirt sleeves would come to the door and ask them what they wanted.

They could not tell what they wanted, they did not know themselves, and the man would use bad language, and slam the door in their faces.

Then they would think that perhaps the Spirit meant the fifth street the other way, or the third house from the opposite corner, and would try again, with still more unpleasant results.

One July I met Whibley, mooning disconsolately along Princes Street, Edinburgh.

"Hullo!" I exclaimed, "what are you doing here? I thought you were busy over that School Board case."

"Yes," he answered, "I ought really to be in London, but the truth is I'm rather expecting something to happen down here."

"Oh!" I said, "and what's that?"

"Well," he replied hesitatingly, as though he would rather not talk about it, "I don't exactly know yet."

"You've come from London to Edinburgh, and don't know what you've come for!" I cried.

"Well, you see," he said, still more reluctantly, as it seemed to me, "it was Maria's idea; she wished —"

"Maria!" I interrupted, looking perhaps a little sternly at him, "who's Maria?" (His wife's name I knew was Emily Georgina Anne.)

"Oh! I forgot," he explained; "she never would tell her name before you, would she? It's the Spirit, you know."

"Oh! that," I said, "it's she that has sent you here. Didn't she tell you what for?"

"No," he answered, "that's what worries me. All she would say was, 'Go to Edinburgh — something will happen.'"

"And how long are you going to remain here?" I inquired.

"I don't know," he replied. "I've been here a week already, and Jobstock writes quite angrily. I wouldn't have come if Maria hadn't been so urgent. She repeated it three evenings running."

I hardly knew what to do. The little man was so dreadfully in earnest about the business that one could not argue much with him.

"You are sure," I said, after thinking a while, "that this Maria is a good Spirit? There are all sorts going about, I'm told. You're sure this isn't the spirit of some deceased lunatic, playing the fool with you?"

"I've thought of that," he admitted. "Of course that might be so. If nothing happens soon I shall almost begin to suspect it."

"Well, I should certainly make some inquiries into its character before I trusted it any further," I answered, and left him.

About a month later I ran against him outside the Law Courts.

"It was all right about Maria; something did happen in Edinburgh while I was there. That very morning I met you one of my oldest clients died quite suddenly at his house at Queensferry, only a few miles outside the city."

"I'm glad of that," I answered, "I mean, of course, for Maria's sake. It was lucky you went then."

"Well, not altogether," he replied, "at least, not in a worldly sense. He left his affairs in a very complicated state, and his eldest son went straight up to London to consult me about them, and, not finding me there, and time being important, went to Kebble. I was rather disappointed when I got back and heard about it."

"Umph!" I said; "she's not a smart spirit, anyway."

"No," he answered, "perhaps not. But, you see, something did really happen."

After that his affection for "Maria" increased tenfold, while her attachment to himself became a burden to his friends. She grew too big for her table, and, dispensing with all mechanical intermediaries, talked to him direct. She followed him everywhere. Mary's lamb couldn't have been a bigger nuisance. She would even go with him into the bedroom, and carry on long conversations with him in the middle of the night. His wife objected; she said it seemed hardly decent, but there was no keeping her out.

She turned up with him at picnics and Christmas parties. Nobody heard her speak to him, but it seemed necessary for him to reply to her aloud, and to see him suddenly get up from his chair and slip away to talk earnestly to nothing in a corner disturbed the festivities.

"I should really be glad," he once confessed to me, "to get a little time to myself. She means kindly, but it *is* a strain. And then the others don't like it. It makes them nervous. I can see it does."

One evening she caused quite a scene at the club. Whibley had been playing whist, with the Major for a partner. At the end of the game the Major, leaning across the table toward him, asked, in a tone of deadly calm, "May I inquire, sir, whether there was any earthly reason" (he emphasised "earthly") "for your following my lead of spades with your only trump?"

"I — I — am very sorry, Major," replied Whibley apologetically. "I — I — somehow felt I — I ought to play that queen."

"Entirely your own inspiration, or suggested?" persisted the Major, who had, of course, heard of "Maria."

Whibley admitted the play had been suggested to him. The Major rose from the table.

"Then, sir," said he, with concentrated indignation, "I decline to continue this game. A human fool I can tolerate for a partner, but if I am to be hampered by a damned spirit —"

"You've no right to say that," cried Whibley hotly.

"I apologise," returned the Major coldly; "we will say a blessed spirit. I decline to play whist with spirits of any kind; and I advise you, sir, if you intend giving many exhibitions with the lady, first to teach her the rudiments of the game."

Saying which the Major put on his hat and left the club, and I made Whibley drink a stiff glass of brandy and water, and sent him and "Maria" home in a cab.

Whibley got rid of "Maria" at last. It cost him in round figures about eight thousand pounds, but his family said it was worth it.

A Spanish Count hired a furnished house a few doors from Whibley's, and one evening he was introduced to Whibley, and came home and had a chat with him. Whibley told him about "Maria," and the Count quite fell in love with her. He said that if only he had had such a spirit to help and advise him, it might have altered his whole life.

He was the first man who had ever said a kind word about the spirit, and Whibley loved him for it. The Count seemed as though he could never see enough of Whibley after that evening, and the three of them — Whibley, the Count, and "Maria" — would sit up half the night talking together.

The precise particulars I never heard. Whibley was always very reticent on the matter. Whether "Maria" really did exist, and the Count deliberately set to work to bamboozle her (she was fool enough for anything), or whether she was a mere hallucination of Whibley's, and the man tricked Whibley by "hypnotic suggestions" (as I believe it is called), I am not prepared to say. The only thing certain is that "Maria" convinced Whibley that the Count had discovered a secret gold mine in Peru. She said she knew all about it, and counselled Whibley to beg the Count to let him put a few thousands into the working of it. "Maria," it appeared, had known the Count from his boyhood, and could answer for it that he was the most honourable man in all South America. Possibly enough he was.

The Count was astonished to find that Whibley knew all about his mine. Eight thousand pounds was needed to start the workings, but he had not mentioned it to any one, as he wanted to keep the whole thing to himself, and thought he could save the money on his estates in Portugal. However, to oblige "Maria," he would let Whibley supply the money. Whibley supplied it — in cash, and no one has ever seen the Count since.

That broke up Whibley's faith in "Maria," and a sensible doctor, getting hold of him threatened to prescribe a lunatic asylum for him if ever he found him carrying on with any spirits again. That completed the cure.

THE MAN WHO WENT WRONG

I first met Jack Burridge nearly ten years ago on a certain North-country race-course.

The saddling bell had just rung for the chief event of the day. I was sauntering along with my hands in my pockets, more interested in the crowd than in the race, when a sporting friend, crossing on his way to the paddock, seized me by the arm and whispered hoarsely in my ear: —

"Put your shirt on Mrs. Waller."

"Put my -?" I began.

"Put your shirt on Mrs. Waller," he repeated still more impressively, and disappeared in the throng.

I stared after him in blank amazement. Why should I put my shirt on Mrs. Waller? Even if it would fit a lady. And how about myself?

I was passing the grand stand, and, glancing up, I saw "Mrs. Waller, twelve to one," chalked on a bookmaker's board. Then it dawned upon me that "Mrs. Waller" was a horse, and, thinking further upon the matter, I evolved the idea that my friend's advice, expressed in more becoming language, was "Back 'Mrs. Waller' for as much as you can possibly afford."

"Thank you," I said to myself, "I have backed cast-iron certainties before. Next time I bet upon a horse I shall make the selection by shutting my eyes and putting a pin through the card."

But the seed had taken root. My friend's words surged in my brain. The birds passing overhead twittered, "Put your shirt on 'Mrs. Waller.'"

I reasoned with myself. I reminded myself of my few former ventures. But the craving to put, if not my shirt, at all events half a sovereign on "Mrs. Waller" only grew the stronger the more strongly I battled against it. I felt that if "Mrs. Waller" won and I had nothing on her, I should reproach myself to my dying day.

I was on the other side of the course. There was no time to get back to the enclosure. The horses were already forming for the start. A few yards off, under a white umbrella, an outside book-maker was shouting his final prices in stentorian tones. He was a big, genial-looking man, with an honest red face.

"What price 'Mrs. Waller'?" I asked him.

"Fourteen to one," he answered, "and good luck to you."

I handed him half a sovereign, and he wrote me out a ticket. I crammed it into my waistcoat pocket, and hurried off to see the race. To my intense astonishment "Mrs. Waller" won. The novel sensation of having backed the winner so excited me that I forgot all about my money, and it was not until a good hour afterwards that I recollected my bet.

Then I started off to search for the man under the white umbrella. I went to where I thought I had left him, but no white umbrella could I find.

Consoling myself with the reflection that my loss served me right for having been fool enough to trust an outside "bookie," I turned on my heel and began to make my way back to my seat. Suddenly a voice hailed me: —

"Here you are, sir. It's Jack Burridge you want. Over here, sir."

I looked round, and there was Jack Burridge at my elbow.

"I saw you looking about, sir," he said, "but I could not make you hear. You was looking the wrong side of the tent."

It was pleasant to find that his honest face had not belied him.

"It is very good of you," I said; "I had given up all hopes of seeing you. Or," I added with a smile, "my seven pounds."

"Seven pun' ten," he corrected me; "you're forgetting your own thin 'un."

He handed me the money and went back to his stand.

On my way into the town I came across him again. A small crowd was collected, thoughtfully watching a tramp knocking about a miserable-looking woman.

Jack, pushing to the front, took in the scene and took off his coat in the same instant.

"Now then, my fine old English gentleman," he sang out, "come and have a try at me for a change."

The tramp was a burly ruffian, and I have seen better boxers than Jack. He got himself a black eye, and a nasty cut over the lip, before he hardly knew where he was. But in spite of that — and a good deal more — he stuck to his man and finished him.

At the end, as he helped his adversary up, I heard him say to the fellow in a kindly whisper: —

"You're too good a sort, you know, to whollop a woman. Why, you very near give me a licking. You must have forgot yourself, matey."

The fellow interested me. I waited and walked on with him. He told me about his home in London, at Mile End — about his old father and mother, his little brothers and sisters — and what he was saving up to do for them. Kindliness oozed from every pore in his skin.

Many that we met knew him, and all, when they saw his round, red face, smiled unconsciously. At the corner of the High Street a pale-faced little drudge of a girl passed us, saying as she slipped by "Good-evening, Mr. Burridge."

He made a dart and caught her by the shoulder.

"And how is father?" he asked.

"Oh, if you please, Mr. Burridge, he is out again. All the mills is closed," answered the child.

"And mother?"

"She don't get no better, sir."

"And who's keeping you all?"

"Oh, if you please, sir, Jimmy's earning something now," replied the mite.

He took a couple of sovereigns from his waistcoat pocket, and closed the child's hand upon them.

"That's all right, my lass, that's all right," he said, stopping her stammering thanks. "You write to me if things don't get better. You know where to find Jack Burridge."

Strolling about the streets in the evening, I happened to pass the inn where he was staying. The parlour window was open, and out into the misty night his deep, cheery voice, trolling forth an old-fashioned drinking song, came rolling like a wind, cleansing the corners of one's heart with its breezy humanness. He was sitting at the head of the table surrounded by a crowd of jovial cronies. I lingered for a while watching the scene. It made the world appear a less sombre dwelling-place than I had sometimes pictured it.

I determined, on my return to London, to look him up, and accordingly one evening started to find the little by-street off the Mile End Road in which he lived. As I turned the corner he drove up in his dog-cart; it was a smart turn-out. On the seat beside him sat a neat, withered little old woman, whom he introduced to me as his mother.

"I tell 'im it's a fine gell as 'e oughter 'ave up 'ere aside 'im," said the old lady, preparing to dismount, "an old woman like me takes all the paint off the show."

"Get along with yer," he replied laughingly, jumping down and handing the reins to the lad who had been waiting, "you could give some of the young uns points yet, mother. I allus promised the old lady as she should ride behind her own 'oss one day," he continued, turning to me, "didn't I, mother?"

"Ay, ay," replied the old soul, as she hobbled nimbly up the steps, "ye're a good son, Jack, ye're a good son."

He led the way into the parlour. As he entered every face lightened up with pleasure, a harmony of joyous welcome greeted him.

The old hard world had been shut out with the slam of the front door. I seemed to have wandered into Dickensland. The red-faced man with the small twinkling eyes and the lungs of leather loomed before me, a large, fat household fairy. From his capacious pockets came forth tobacco for the old father; a huge bunch of hot-house grapes for a neighbour's sickly child, who was stopping with them; a book of Henty's — beloved of boys — for a noisy youngster who called him "uncle"; a bottle of port wine for a wan, elderly woman with a swollen face — his widowed sister-in-law, as I subsequently learned; sweets enough for the baby (whose baby I don't know) to make it sick for a week; and a roll of music for his youngest sister.

"We're a-going to make a lady of her," he said, drawing the child's shy face against his gaudy waistcoat, and running his coarse hand through her pretty curls; "and she shall marry a jockey when she grows up."

After supper he brewed some excellent whisky punch, and insisted upon the old lady joining us, which she eventually did with much coughing and protestation; but I noticed that she finished the tumblerful. For the children he concocted a marvellous mixture, which he called an "eye-composer," the chief ingredients being hot lemonade, ginger wine, sugar, oranges, and raspberry vinegar. It had the desired effect.

I stayed till late, listening to his inexhaustible fund of stories. Over most of them he laughed with us himself — a great gusty laugh that made the cheap glass ornaments upon the mantelpiece to tremble; but now and then a recollection came to him that spread a sudden gravity across his jovial face, bringing a curious quaver into his deep voice.

Their tongues a little loosened by the punch, the old folks would have sung his praises to the verge of tediousness had he not almost sternly interrupted them.

"Shut up, mother," he cried at last, quite gruffly, "what I does I does to please myself. I likes to see people comfortable about me. If they wasn't, it's me as would be more upset than them."

I did not see him again for nearly two years. Then one October evening, strolling about the East End, I met him coming out of a little Chapel in the Burdett Road. He was so changed that I should not have known him had not I overheard a woman as she passed him say, "Good-evening, Mr. Burridge."

A pair of bushy side-whiskers had given to his red face an aggressively respectable appearance. He was dressed in an ill-fitting suit of black, and carried an umbrella in one hand and a book in the other.

In some mysterious way he managed to look both thinner and shorter than my recollection of him. Altogether, he suggested to me the idea that he himself — the real man — had by some means or other been extracted, leaving only his shrunken husk behind. The genial juices of humanity had been squeezed out of him.

"Not Jack Burridge!" I exclaimed, confronting him in astonishment.

His little eyes wandered shiftily up and down the street. "No, sir," he replied (his tones had lost their windy boisterousness — a hard, metallic voice spoke to me), "not the one as you used to know, praise be the Lord."

"And have you given up the old business?" I asked.

"Yes, sir," he replied, "that's all over; I've been a vile sinner in my time, God forgive me for it. But, thank Heaven, I have repented in time."

"Come and have a drink," I said, slipping my arm through his, "and tell me all about it."

He disengaged himself from me, firmly but gently. "You mean well, sir," he said, "but I have given up the drink."

Evidently he would have been rid of me, but a literary man, scenting material for his stockpot, is not easily shaken off. I asked after the old folks, and if they were still stopping with him.

"Yes," he said, "for the present. Of course, a man can't be expected to keep people for ever; so many mouths to fill is hard work these times, and everybody sponges on a man just because he's good-natured."

"And how are you getting on?" I asked.

"Tolerably well, thank you, sir. The Lord provides for His servants," he replied with a smug smile. "I have got a little shop now in the Commercial Road."

"Whereabouts?" I persisted. "I would like to call and see you."

He gave me the address reluctantly, and said he would esteem it a great pleasure if I would honour him by a visit, which was a palpable lie.

The following afternoon I went. I found the place to be a pawnbroker's shop, and from all appearances he must have been doing a very brisk business. He was out himself attending a temperance committee, but his old father was behind the counter, and asked me inside. Though it was a chilly day there was no fire in the parlour, and the two old folks sat one each side of the empty hearth, silent and sad. They seemed little more pleased to see me than their son, but after a while Mrs. Burridge's natural garrulity asserted itself, and we fell into chat.

I asked what had become of his sister-in-law, the lady with the swollen face.

"I couldn't rightly tell you, sir," answered the old lady, "she ain't livin' with us now. You see, sir," she continued, "John's got different notions to what 'e used to 'ave. 'E don't cotten much to them as ain't found grace, and poor Jane never did 'ave much religion!"

"And the little one?" I inquired. "The one with the curls?"

"What, Bessie, sir?" said the old lady. "Oh, she's out at service, sir; John don't think it good for young folks to be idle."

"Your son seems to have changed a good deal, Mrs. Burridge," I remarked.

"Ay, sir," she assented, "you may well say that. It nearly broke my 'art at fust; everythin' so different to what it 'ad been. Not as I'd stand in the boy's light. If our being a bit uncomfortable like in this world is a-going to do 'im any good in the next me and father ain't the ones to begrudge it, are we, old man?"

The "old man" concurred grumpily.

"Was it a sudden conversion?" I asked. "How did it come about?"

"It was a young woman as started 'im off," explained the old lady. "She come round to our place one day a-collectin' for somethin' or other, and Jack, in 'is free-'anded way, 'e give 'er a five-pun' note. Next week she come agen for somethin' else, and stopped and talked to 'im about 'is soul in the passage. She told 'im as 'e was a-goin' straight to 'ell, and that 'e oughter give up the bookmakin' and settle down to a respec'ble, God-fearin' business. At fust 'e only laughed, but she lammed in tracts at 'im full of the most awful language; and one day she fetched 'im round to one of them revivalist chaps, as fair settled 'im.

"'E ain't never been his old self since then. 'E give up the bettin' and bought this 'ere, though what's the difference blessed if I can see. It makes my 'eart ache, it do, to 'ear my Jack a-beatin' down the poor people — and it ain't like 'im. It went agen 'is grain at fust, I could see; but they told him as 'ow it was folks's own fault that they was poor, and as 'ow it was the will of God, because they was a drinkin', improvident lot.

"Then they made 'im sign the pledge. 'E'd allus been used to 'is glass, Jack 'ad, and I think as knockin' it off 'ave soured 'im a bit — seems as if all the sperit 'ad gone out of 'im — and of course me and father 'ave 'ad to give up our little drop too. Then they told 'im as 'e must give up smokin'- that was another way of goin' straight to 'ell — and that ain't made 'im any the more cheerful like, and father misses 'is little bit — don't ye, father?"

"Ay," answered the old fellow savagely; "can't say I thinks much of these 'ere folks as is going to heaven; blowed if I don't think they'll be a chirpier lot in t'other place."

An angry discussion in the shop interrupted us. Jack had returned, and was threatening an excited woman with the police. It seemed she had miscalculated the date, and had come a day too late with her interest.

Having got rid of her, he came into the parlour with the watch in his hand.

"It's providential she was late," he said, looking at it; "it's worth ten times what I lent on it."

He packed his father back into the shop, and his mother down into the kitchen to get his tea, and for a while we sat together talking.

I found his conversation a strange mixture of self-laudation, showing through a flimsy veil of self-disparagement, and of satisfaction at the conviction that he was "saved," combined with equally evident satisfaction that most other people weren't — somewhat trying, however; and, remembering an appointment, rose to go.

He made no effort to stay me, but I could see that he was bursting to tell me something. At last, taking a religious paper from his pocket, and pointing to a column, he blurted out:

"You don't take any interest in the Lord's vineyard, I suppose, sir?"

I glanced at the part of the paper indicated. It announced a new mission to the Chinese, and heading the subscription list stood the name, "Mr. John Burridge, one hundred guineas."

"You subscribe largely, Mr. Burridge," I said, handing him back the paper.

He rubbed his big hands together. "The Lord will repay a hundredfold," he answered.

"In which case it's just as well to have a note of the advance down in black and white, eh?" I added.

His little eyes looked sharply at me; but he made no reply, and, shaking hands, I left him.

THE HOBBY RIDER

Bump. Bump. Bump-bump. Bump.

I sat up in bed and listened intently. It seemed to me as if someone with a muffled hammer were trying to knock bricks out of the wall.

"Burglars," I said to myself (one assumes, as a matter of course, that everything happening in this world after 1 a.m. is due to burglars), and I reflected what a curiously literal, but at the same time slow and cumbersome, method of housebreaking they had adopted.

The bumping continued irregularly, yet uninterruptedly.

My bed was by the window. I reached out my hand and drew aside a corner of the curtain. The sunlight streamed into the room. I looked at my watch: it was ten minutes past five.

A most unbusinesslike hour for burglars, I thought. Why, it will be breakfast-time before they get in.

Suddenly there came a crash, and some substance striking against the blind fell upon the floor. I sprang out of bed and threw open the window.

A red-haired young gentleman, scantily clad in a sweater and a pair of flannel trousers, stood on the lawn below me.

"Good morning," he said cheerily. "Do you mind throwing me back my ball?"

"What ball?" I said.

"My tennis ball," he answered. "It must be somewhere in the room; it went clean through the window."

I found the ball and threw it back to him,

"What are you doing?" I asked. "Playing tennis?"

"No," he said. "I am just practising against the side of the house. It improves your game wonderfully."

"It don't improve my night's rest," I answered somewhat surlily I fear. "I came down here for peace and quiet. Can't you do it in the daytime?"

"Daytime!" he laughed. "Why it has been daytime for the last two hours. Never mind, I'll go round the other side."

He disappeared round the corner, and set to work at the back, where he woke up the dog. I heard another window smash, followed by a sound as of somebody getting up violently in a distant part of the house, and shortly afterwards I must have fallen asleep again.

I had come to spend a few weeks at a boarding establishment in

Deal. He was the only other young man in the house, and I was naturally thrown a good deal upon his society. He was a pleasant, genial young fellow, but he would have been better company had he been a little less enthusiastic as regards tennis.

He played tennis ten hours a day on the average. He got up romantic parties to play it by moonlight (when half his time was generally taken up in separating his opponents), and godless parties to play it on Sundays. On wet days I have seen him practising services by himself in a mackintosh and goloshes.

He had been spending the winter with his people at Tangiers, and I asked him how he liked the place.

"Oh, a beast of a hole!" he replied. "There is not a court anywhere in the town. We tried playing on the roof, but the *mater* thought it dangerous."

Switzerland he had been delighted with. He counselled me next time I went to stay at Zermatt.

"There is a capital court at Zermatt," he said. "You might almost fancy yourself at Wimbledon."

A mutual acquaintance whom I subsequently met told me that at the top of the Jungfrau he had said to him, his eyes fixed the while upon a small snow plateau enclosed by precipices a few hundred feet below them —

"By Jove! That wouldn't make half a bad little tennis court — that flat bit down there. Have to be careful you didn't run back too far."

When he was not playing tennis, or practising tennis, or reading about tennis, he was talking about tennis. Renshaw was the prominent figure in the tennis world at that time, and he mentioned Renshaw until there grew up within my soul a dark desire to kill Renshaw in a quiet, unostentatious way, and bury him.

One drenching afternoon he talked tennis to me for three hours on end, referring to Renshaw, so far as I kept count, four thousand nine hundred and thirteen times. After tea he drew his chair to the window beside me, and commenced —

"Have you ever noticed how Renshaw —"

I said —

"Suppose someone took a gun — someone who could aim very straight — and went out and shot Renshaw till he was quite dead, would you tennis players drop him and talk about somebody else?"

"Oh, but who would shoot Renshaw?" he said indignantly.

"Never mind," I said, "supposing someone did?"

"Well, then, there would be his brother," he replied.

I had forgotten that.

"Well, we won't argue about how many of them there are," I said. "Suppose someone killed the lot, should we hear less of Renshaw?"

"Never," he replied emphatically. "Renshaw will always be a name wherever tennis is spoken of."

I dread to think what the result might have been had his answer been other than it was.

The next year he dropped tennis completely and became an ardent amateur photographer, whereupon all his friends implored him to return to tennis, and sought to interest him in talk about services and returns and volleys, and in anecdotes concerning Renshaw. But he would not heed them.

Whatever he saw, wherever he went, he took. He took his friends, and made them his enemies. He took babies, and brought despair to fond mothers' hearts. He took young wives, and cast a shadow on the home. Once there was a young man who loved not wisely, so his friends thought, but the more they talked against her the more he clung to her. Then a happy idea occurred to the father. He got Begglely to photograph her in seven different positions.

When her lover saw the first, he said ──

"What an awful looking thing! Who did it?"

When Begglely showed him the second, he said ──

"But, my dear fellow, it's not a bit like her. You've made her look an ugly old woman."

At the third he said ──

"Whatever have you done to her feet? They can't be that size, you know. It isn't in nature!"

At the fourth he exclaimed ──

"But, heavens, man! Look at the shape you've made her. Where on earth did you get the idea from?"

At the first glimpse of the fifth he staggered.

"Great Scott!" he cried with a shudder, "what a ghastly expression you've got into it! It isn't human!"

Begglely was growing offended, but the father, who was standing by, came to his defence.

"It's nothing to do with Begglely," exclaimed the old gentleman suavely. "It can't be *his* fault. What is a photographer? Simply an instrument in the hands of science. He arranges his apparatus, and whatever is in front of it comes into it."

"No," continued the old gentleman, laying a constrained hand upon Begglely, who was about to resume the exhibition, "don't ── don't show him the other two."

I was sorry for the poor girl, for I believe she really cared for the youngster; and as for her looks, they were quite up to the average. But some evil sprite seemed to have got into Begglely's camera. It seized upon defects with the unerring instinct of a born critic, and dilated upon them to the obscuration of all virtues. A man with a pimple became a pimple with a man as background. People with strongly marked features became merely adjuncts to their own noses. One man in the neighbourhood had, undetected, worn a wig for fourteen years. Begglely's camera discovered the fraud in an instant, and so completely exposed it that the man's friends wondered afterwards how the fact ever could have escaped them. The thing seemed to take a pleasure in showing humanity at its very worst. Babies usually came out with an expression of low cunning. Most young girls had to take their choice of appearing either as simpering idiots or embryo vixens. To mild old ladies it generally gave a look of aggressive cynicism. Our vicar, as excellent an old gentleman as ever breathed, Begglely presented to us as a beetle-browed savage of a peculiarly low type of intellect; while upon the leading solicitor of the town he bestowed an expression of such thinly-veiled hypocrisy that few who saw the photograph cared ever again to trust him with their affairs.

As regards myself I should, perhaps, make no comment, I am possibly a prejudiced party. All I will say, therefore, is that if I in any way resemble Begglely's photograph of me, then the critics are fully justified in everything they have at any time, anywhere, said of me — and more. Nor, I maintain — though I make no pretence of possessing the figure of Apollo — is one of my legs twice the length of the other, and neither does it curve upwards. This I can prove. Begglely allowed that an accident had occurred to the negative during the process of development, but this explanation does not appear on the picture, and I cannot help feeling that an injustice has been done me.

His perspective seemed to be governed by no law either human or divine. I have seen a photograph of his uncle and a windmill, judging from which I defy any unprejudiced person to say which is the bigger, the uncle or the mill.

On one occasion he created quite a scandal in the parish by exhibiting a well-known and eminently respectable maiden lady nursing a young man on her knee. The gentleman's face was indistinct, and he was dressed in a costume which, upon a man of his size — one would have estimated him as rising 6 ft. 4 in. — appeared absurdly juvenile. He had one arm round her neck, and she was holding his other hand and smirking.

I, knowing something of Begglely's machine, willingly accepted the lady's explanation, which was to the effect that the male in question was her nephew, aged eleven; but the uncharitable ridiculed this statement, and appearances were certainly against her.

It was in the early days of the photographic craze, and an inexperienced world was rather pleased with the idea of being taken on the cheap. The consequence was that nearly everyone for three miles round sat or stood or leant or laid to Begglely at one time or another, with the result that a less conceited parish than ours it would have been difficult to discover. No one who had once looked upon a photograph of himself taken by Begglely ever again felt any pride in his personal appearance. The picture was invariably a revelation to him.

Later, some evil-disposed person invented Kodaks, and Begglely went everywhere slung on to a thing that looked like an overgrown missionary box, and that bore a legend to the effect that if Begglely would pull the button, a shameless Company would do the rest. Life became a misery to Begglely's friends. Nobody dared to do anything for fear of being taken in the act. He took an instantaneous photograph of his own father swearing at the gardener, and snapped his youngest sister and her lover at the exact moment of farewell at the garden gate. Nothing was sacred to him. He Kodaked his aunt's funeral from behind, and showed the chief mourner but one whispering a funny story into the ear of the third cousin as they stood behind their hats beside the grave.

Public indignation was at its highest when a new comer to the neighbourhood, a young fellow named Haynoth, suggested the getting together of a party for a summer's tour in Turkey. Everybody took up the idea with enthusiasm, and recommended Begglely as the "party." We had great hopes from that tour. Our idea was that Begglely would pull his button outside a harem or behind a sultana, and that a Bashi Bazouk or a Janissary would do the rest for us.

We were, however, partly doomed to disappointment — I say, "partly," because, although Begglely returned alive, he came back entirely cured of his photographic craze. He said that every English-speaking man, woman, or child whom he met abroad had its camera with it, and that after a time the sight of a black cloth or the click of a button began to madden him.

He told us that on the summit of Mount Tutra, in the Carpathians, the English and American amateur photographers waiting to take "the grand panorama" were formed by the Hungarian police in queue, two abreast, each with his or her camera under his or her arm, and that a man had to stand sometimes as long as three and a half hours before his turn came round. He also told us that the beggars in Constantinople went about with placards hung round their necks, stating their charges for being photographed. One of these price lists he brought back with him as a sample.

It ran: —

One snap shot, back or front	. . . . 2 frcs.
" with expression	. . . . 3 frcs.
" surprised in quaint attitude.	. . . . 4 frcs.
" while saying prayers	. . . . 5 frcs.
" while fighting	. . . . 10 frcs.

He said that in some instances where a man had an exceptionally villainous cast of countenance, or was exceptionally deformed, as much as twenty francs were demanded and readily obtained.

He abandoned photography and took to golf. He showed people how, by digging a hole here and putting a brickbat or two there, they could convert a tennis-lawn into a miniature golf link, — and did it for them. He persuaded elderly ladies and gentlemen that it was the mildest exercise going, and would drag them for miles over wet gorse and heather, and bring them home dead beat, coughing, and full of evil thoughts.

The last time I saw him was in Switzerland, a few months ago. He appeared indifferent to the subject of golf, but talked much about whist. We met by chance at Grindelwald, and agreed to climb the Faulhorn together next morning. Half-way up we rested, and I strolled on a little way by myself to gain a view. Returning, I found him with a "Cavendish" in his hand and a pack of cards spread out before him on the grass, solving a problem.

THE MAN WHO DID NOT BELIEVE IN LUCK

He got in at Ipswich with seven different weekly papers under his arm. I noticed that each one insured its reader against death or injury by railway accident. He arranged his luggage upon the rack above him, took off his hat and laid it on the seat beside him, mopped his bald head with a red silk handkerchief, and then set to work steadily to write his name and address upon each of the seven papers. I sat opposite to him and read *Punch*. I always take the old humour when travelling; I find it soothing to the nerves.

Passing over the points at Manningtree the train gave a lurch, and a horse-shoe he had carefully placed in the rack above him slipped through the netting, falling with a musical ring upon his head.

He appeared neither surprised nor angry. Having staunched the wound with his handkerchief, he stooped and picked the horse-shoe up, glanced at it with, as I thought, an expression of reproach, and dropped it gently out of the window.

"Did it hurt you?" I asked.

It was a foolish question. I told myself so the moment I had uttered it. The thing must have weighed three pounds at the least; it was an exceptionally large and heavy shoe. The bump on his head was swelling visibly before my eyes. Anyone but an idiot must have seen that he was hurt. I expected an irritable reply. I should have given one myself had I been in his place. Instead, however, he seemed to regard the inquiry as a natural and kindly expression of sympathy.

"It did, a little," he replied.

"What were you doing with it?" I asked. It was an odd sort of thing for a man to be travelling with.

"It was lying in the roadway just outside the station," he explained; "I picked it up for luck."

He refolded his handkerchief so as to bring a cooler surface in contact with the swelling, while I murmured something genial about the inscrutability of Providence.

"Yes," he said, "I've had a deal of luck in my time, but it's never turned out well."

"I was born on a Wednesday," he continued, "which, as I daresay you know, is the luckiest day a man can be born on. My mother was a widow, and none of my relatives would do anything for me. They said it would be like taking coals to Newcastle, helping a boy born on a Wednesday; and my uncle, when he died, left every penny of his money to my brother Sam, as a slight compensation to him for having been born on a Friday. All I ever got was advice upon the duties and responsibilities of wealth, when it arrived, and entreaties that I would not neglect those with claims upon me when I came to be a rich man."

He paused while folding up his various insurance papers and placing them in the inside breast-pocket of his coat.

"Then there are black cats," he went on; "they're said to be lucky. Why, there never was a blacker cat than the one that followed me into my rooms in Bolsover Street the very first night I took them."

"Didn't it bring you luck?" I enquired, finding that he had stopped.

A far-away look came into his eyes.

"Well, of course it all depends," he answered dreamily. "Maybe we'd never have suited one another; you can always look at it that way. Still, I'd like to have tried."

He sat staring out of the window, and for a while I did not care to intrude upon his evidently painful memories.

"What happened then?" I asked, however, at last.

He roused himself from his reverie.

"Oh," he said. "Nothing extraordinary. She had to leave London for a time, and gave me her pet canary to take charge of while she was away."

"But it wasn't your fault," I urged.

"No, perhaps not," he agreed; "but it created a coldness which others were not slow to take advantage of."

"I offered her the cat, too," he added, but more to himself than to me.

We sat and smoked in silence. I felt that the consolations of a stranger would sound weak.

"Piebald horses are lucky, too," he observed, knocking the ashes from his pipe against the window sash. "I had one of them once."

"What did it do to you?" I enquired.

"Lost me the best crib I ever had in my life," was the simple rejoinder. "The governor stood it a good deal longer than I had any right to expect; but you can't keep a man who is *always* drunk. It gives a firm a bad name."

"It would," I agreed.

"You see," he went on, "I never had the head for it. To some men it would not have so much mattered, but the very first glass was enough to upset me. I'd never been used to it."

"But why did you take it?" I persisted. "The horse didn't make you drink, did he?"

"Well, it was this way," he explained, continuing to rub gently the lump which was now about the size of an egg. "The animal had belonged to a gentleman who travelled in the wine and spirit line, and who had been accustomed to visit in the way of business almost every public-house he came to. The result was you couldn't get that little horse past a public-house — at least I couldn't. He sighted them a quarter of a mile off, and made straight for the door. I struggled with him at first, but it was five to ten minutes' work getting him away, and folks used to gather round and bet on us. I think, maybe, I'd have stuck to it, however, if it hadn't been for a temperance chap who stopped one day and lectured the crowd about it from the opposite side of the street. He called me Pilgrim, and said the little horse was 'Pollion,' or some such name, and kept on shouting out that I was to fight him for a heavenly crown. After that they called us "Polly and the Pilgrim, fighting for the crown." It riled me, that did, and at the very next house at which he pulled up I got down and said I'd come for two of Scotch. That was the beginning. It took me years to break myself of the habit.

"But there," he continued, "it has always been the same. I hadn't been a fortnight in my first situation before my employer gave me a goose weighing eighteen pounds as a Christmas present."

"Well, that couldn't have done you any harm," I remarked. "That was lucky enough."

"So the other clerks said at the time," he replied. "The old gentleman had never been known to give anything away before in his life. 'He's taken a fancy to you,' they said; 'you are a lucky beggar!'"

He sighed heavily. I felt there was a story attached.

"What did you do with it?" I asked.

"That was the trouble," he returned. "I didn't know what to do with it. It was ten o'clock on Christmas Eve, just as I was leaving, that he gave it to me. 'Tiddling Brothers have sent me a goose, Biggles,' he said to me as I helped him on with his great-coat. 'Very kind of 'em, but I don't want it myself; you can have it!'

"Of course I thanked him, and was very grateful. He wished me a merry Christmas and went out. I tied the thing up in brown paper, and took it under my arm. It was a fine bird, but heavy.

"Under all the circumstances, and it being Christmas time, I thought I would treat myself to a glass of beer. I went into a quiet little house at the corner of the Lane and laid the goose on the counter.

"'That's a big 'un,' said the landlord; 'you'll get a good cut off him to-morrow.'

"His words set me thinking, and for the first time it struck me that I didn't want the bird — that it was of no use to me at all. I was going down to spend the holidays with my young lady's people in Kent."

"Was this the canary young lady?" I interrupted.

"No," he replied. "This was before that one. It was this goose I'm telling you of that upset this one. Well, her folks were big farmers; it would have been absurd taking a goose down to them, and I knew no one in London to give it to, so when the landlord came round again I asked him if he would care to buy it. I told him he could have it cheap,

"'I don't want it myself,' he answered. 'I've got three in the house already. Perhaps one of these gentlemen would like to make an offer.'

"He turned to a couple of chaps who were sitting drinking gin. They didn't look to me worth the price of a chicken between them. The seediest said he'd like to look at it, however, and I undid the parcel. He mauled the thing pretty considerably, and cross-exam-ined me as to how I come by it, ending by upsetting half a tumbler of gin and water over it. Then he offered me half a crown for it. It made me so angry that I took the brown paper and the string in one hand and the goose in the other, and walked straight out without saying a word.

"I carried it in this way for some distance, because I was excited and didn't care how I carried it; but as I cooled, I began to reflect how ridiculous I must look. One or two small boys evidently no-ticed the same thing. I stopped under a lamp-post and tried to tie it up again. I had a bag and an umbrella with me at the same time, and the first thing I did was to drop the goose into the gutter, which is just what I might have expected to do, attempting to handle four separate articles and three yards of string with one pair of hands. I picked up about a quart of mud with that goose, and got the greater part of it over my hands and clothes and a fair quantity over the brown paper; and then it began to rain.

"I bundled everything up into my arm and made for the nearest pub, where I thought I would ask for a piece more string and make a neat job of it.

"The bar was crowded. I pushed my way to the counter and flung the goose down in front of me. The men nearest stopped talking to look at it; and a young fellow standing next to me said —

"'Well, you've killed it.' I daresay I did seem a bit excited.

"I had intended making another effort to sell it here, but they were clearly not the right sort. I had a pint of ale — for I was feeling somewhat tired and hot — scraped as much of the mud off the bird as I could, made a fresh parcel of it, and came out.

"Crossing the road a happy idea occurred to me. I thought I would raffle it. At once I set to work to find a house where there might seem to be a likely lot. It cost me three or four whiskies — for I felt I didn't want any more beer, which is a thing that easily upsets me — but at length I found just the crowd I wanted — a quiet domestic-looking set in a homely little place off the Goswell Road.

"I explained my views to the landlord. He said he had no objection; he supposed I would stand drinks round afterwards. I said I should be delighted to do so, and showed him the bird.

"'It looks a bit poorly,' he said. He was a Devonshire man.

"'Oh, that's nothing,' I explained. 'I happened to drop it. That will all wash off.'

"'It smells a bit queer, too,' he said.

"'That's mud,' I answered; 'you know what London mud is. And a gentleman spilled some gin over it. Nobody will notice that when it's cooked.'

"'Well,' he replied. 'I don't think I'll take a hand myself, but if any other gent likes to, that's his affair.'

"Nobody seemed enthusiastic. I started it at sixpence, and took a ticket myself. The potman had a free chance for superintending the arrangements, and he succeeded in inducing five other men, much against their will, to join us. I won it myself, and paid out three and twopence for drinks. A solemn-looking individual who had been snoring in a corner suddenly woke up as I was going out, and offered me sevenpence ha'penny for it — why sevenpence ha'penny I have never been able to understand. He would have taken it away, I should never have seen it again, and my whole life might have been different. But Fate has always been against me. I replied, with perhaps unnecessary hauteur, that I wasn't a Christmas dinner fund for the destitute, and walked out.

"It was getting late, and I had a long walk home to my lodgings. I was beginning to wish I had never seen the bird. I estimated its weight by this time to be thirty-six pounds.

"The idea occurred to me to sell it to a poulterer. I looked for a shop, I found one in Myddleton Street. There wasn't a customer near it, but by the way the man was shouting you might have thought that he was doing all the trade of Clerkenwell. I took the goose out of the parcel and laid it on the shelf before him.

"'What's this?' he asked.

"'It's a goose,' I said. 'You can have it cheap.'

"He just seized the thing by the neck and flung it at me. I dodged, and it caught the side of my head. You can have no idea, if you've never been hit on the head with a goose, how if hurts. I picked it up and hit him back with it, and a policeman came up with the usual, 'Now then, what's all this about?'

"I explained the facts. The poulterer stepped to the edge of the curb and apostrophised the universe generally.

"'Look at that shop,' he said. 'It's twenty minutes to twelve, and there's seven dozen geese hanging there that I'm willing to give away, and this fool asks me if I want to buy another.'

"I perceived then that my notion had been a foolish one, and I followed the policeman's advice, and went away quietly, taking the bird with me.

"Then said I to myself, 'I will give it away. I will select some poor deserving person, and make him a present of the damned thing.' I passed a good many people, but no one looked deserving enough. It may have been the time or it may have been the neighbourhood, but those I met seemed to me to be unworthy of the bird. I offered it to a man in Judd Street, who I thought appeared hungry. He turned out to be a drunken ruffian. I could not make him understand what I meant, and he followed me down the road abusing me at the top of his voice, until, turning a corner without knowing it, he plunged down Tavistock Place, shouting after the wrong man. In the Euston Road I stopped a half-starved child and pressed it upon her. She answered 'Not me!' and ran away. I heard her calling shrilly after me, 'Who stole the goose?'

"I dropped it in a dark part of Seymour Street. A man picked it up and brought it after me. I was unequal to any more explanations or arguments. I gave him twopence and plodded on with it once more. The pubs were just closing, and I went into one for a final drink. As a matter of fact I had had enough already, being, as I am, unaccustomed to anything more than an occasional class of beer. But I felt depressed, and I thought it might cheer me. I think I had gin, which is a thing I loathe.

"I meant to fling it over into Oakley Square, but a policeman had his eye on me, and followed me twice round the railings. In Golding Road I sought to throw it down an area, but was frustrated in like manner. The whole night police of London seemed to have nothing else to do but prevent my getting rid of that goose.

"They appeared so anxious about it that I fancied they might like to have it. I went up to one in Camden Street. I called him 'Bobby,' and asked him if he wanted a goose.

"'I'll tell you what I don't want,' he replied severely, 'and that is none of your sauce.'

"He was very insulting, and I naturally answered him back.

What actually passed I forget, but it ended in his announcing his intention of taking me in charge.

"I slipped out of his hands and bolted down King Street. He blew his whistle and started after me. A man sprang out from a doorway in College Street and tried to stop me. I tied him up with a butt in the stomach, and cut through the Crescent, doubling back into the Camden Road by Batt Street.

"At the Canal Bridge I looked behind me, and could see no one. I dropped the goose over the parapet, and it fell with a splash into the water.

"Heaving a sigh of relief, I turned and crossed into Randolph Street, and there a constable collared me. I was arguing with him when the first fool came up breathless. They told me I had better explain the matter to the Inspector, and I thought so too.

"The Inspector asked me why I had run away when the other constable wanted to take me in charge. I replied that it was because I did not desire to spend my Christmas holidays in the lock-up, which he evidently regarded as a singularly weak argument. He asked me what I had thrown into the canal. I told him a goose. He asked me why I had thrown a goose into the canal. I told him because I was sick and tired of the animal.

"At this stage a sergeant came in to say that they had succeeded in recovering the parcel. They opened it on the Inspector's table. It contained a dead baby.

"I pointed out to them that it wasn't my parcel, and that it wasn't my baby, but they hardly took the trouble to disguise the fact that they did not believe me.

"The Inspector said it was too grave a case for bail, which, seeing that I did not know a soul in London, was somewhat immaterial. I got them to send a telegram to my young lady to say that I was unavoidably detained in town, and passed as quiet and uneventful a Christmas Day and Boxing Day as I ever wish to spend.

"In the end the evidence against me was held to be insufficient to justify a conviction, and I got off on the minor charge of drunk and disorderly. But I lost my situation and I lost my young lady, and I don't care if I never see a goose again."

We were nearing Liverpool Street. He collected his luggage, and taking up his hat made an attempt to put it on his head. But in consequence of the swelling caused by the horseshoe it would not go anywhere near him, and he laid it sadly back upon the seat.

"No," he said quietly, "I can't say that I believe very much in luck."

DICK DUNKERMAN'S CAT

Richard Dunkerman and I had been old school-fellows, if a gentleman belonging to the Upper Sixth, and arriving each morning in a "topper" and a pair of gloves, and "a discredit to the Lower Fourth," in a Scotch cap, can by any manner of means be classed together. And though in those early days a certain amount of coldness existed between us, originating in a poem, composed and sung on occasions by myself in commemoration of an alleged painful incident connected with a certain breaking-up day, and which, if I remember rightly ran: —

Dicky, Dicky, Dunk,
Always in a funk,
Drank a glass of sherry wine,
And went home roaring drunk,

and kept alive by his brutal criticism of the same, expressed with the bony part of the knee, yet in after life we came to know and like each other better. I drifted into journalism, while he for years had been an unsuccessful barrister and dramatist; but one spring, to the astonishment of us all, he brought out the play of the season, a somewhat impossible little comedy, but full of homely sentiment and belief in human nature. It was about a couple of months after its production that he first introduced me to "Pyramids, Esquire."

I was in love at the time. Her name was, I think, Naomi, and I wanted to talk to somebody about her. Dick had a reputation for taking an intelligent interest in other men's love affairs. He would let a lover rave by the hour to him, taking brief notes the while in a bulky red-covered volume labelled "Commonplace Book." Of course everybody knew that he was using them merely as raw material for his dramas, but we did not mind that so long as he would only listen. I put on my hat and went round to his chambers.

We talked about indifferent matters for a quarter of an hour or so, and then I launched forth upon my theme. I had exhausted her beauty and goodness, and was well into my own feelings — the madness of my ever imagining I had loved before, the utter impossibility of my ever caring for any other woman, and my desire to die breathing her name — before he made a move. I thought he had risen to reach down, as usual, the "Commonplace Book," and so waited, but instead he went to the door and opened it, and in glided one of the largest and most beautiful black tom-cats I have ever seen. It sprang on Dick's knee with a soft "cur-roo," and sat there upright, watching me, and I went on with my tale.

After a few minutes Dick interrupted me with: ——

"I thought you said her name was Naomi?"

"So it is," I replied. "Why?"

"Oh, nothing," he answered, "only just now you referred to her as Enid."

This was remarkable, as I had not seen Enid for years, and had quite forgotten her. Somehow it took the glitter out of the conversation. A dozen sentences later Dick stopped me again with: ——

"Who's Julia?"

I began to get irritated. Julia, I remembered, had been cashier in a city restaurant, and had, when I was little more than a boy, almost inveigled me into an engagement. I found myself getting hot at the recollection of the spooney rhapsodies I had hoarsely poured into her powder-streaked ear while holding her flabby hand across the counter.

"Did I really say 'Julia'?" I answered somewhat sharply, "or are you joking?"

"You certainly alluded to her as Julia," he replied mildly. "But never mind, you go on as you like, I shall know whom you mean."

But the flame was dead within me. I tried to rekindle it, but every time I glanced up and met the green eyes of the black Tom it flickered out again. I recalled the thrill that had penetrated my whole being when Naomi's hand had accidently touched mine in the conservatory, and wondered whether she had done it on purpose. I thought how good and sweet she was to that irritatingly silly old frump her mother, and wondered if it really were her mother, or only hired. I pictured her crown of gold-brown hair as I had last seen it with the sunlight kissing its wanton waves, and felt I would like to be quite sure that it were all her own.

Once I clutched the flying skirts of my enthusiasm with sufficient firmness to remark that in my own private opinion a good woman was more precious than rubies; adding immediately afterwards — the words escaping me unconsciously before I was aware even of the thought — "pity it's so difficult to tell 'em."

Then I gave it up, and sat trying to remember what I had said to her the evening before, and hoping I had not committed myself.

Dick's voice roused me from my unpleasant reverie.

"No," he said, "I thought you would not be able to. None of them can."

"None of them can what?" I asked. Somehow I was feeling angry with Dick and with Dick's cat, and with myself and most other things.

"Why talk love or any other kind of sentiment before old Pyramids here?" he replied, stroking the cat's soft head as it rose and arched its back.

"What's the confounded cat got to do with it?" I snapped.

"That's just what I can't tell you," he answered, "but it's very remarkable. Old Leman dropped in here the other evening and began in his usual style about Ibsen and the destiny of the human race, and the Socialistic idea and all the rest of it — you know his way. Pyramids sat on the edge of the table there and looked at him, just as he sat looking at you a few minutes ago, and in less than a quarter of an hour Leman had come to the conclusion that society would do better without ideals and that the destiny of the human race was in all probability the dust heap. He pushed his long hair back from his eyes and looked, for the first time in his life, quite sane. 'We talk about ourselves,' he said, 'as though we were the end of creation. I get tired listening to myself sometimes. Pah!' he continued, 'for all we know the human race may die out utterly and another insect take our place, as possibly we pushed out and took the place of a former race of beings. I wonder if the ant tribe may not be the future inheritors of the earth. They understand combination, and already have an extra sense that we lack. If in the courses of evolution they grow bigger in brain and body, they may become powerful rivals, who knows?' Curious to hear old Leman talking like that, wasn't it?"

"What made you call him 'Pyramids'?" I asked of Dick.

"I don't know," he answered, "I suppose because he looked so old. The name came to me."

I leaned across and looked into the great green eyes, and the creature, never winking, never blinking, looked back into mine, until the feeling came to me that I was being drawn down into the very wells of time. It seemed as though the panorama of the ages must have passed in review before those expressionless orbs — all the loves and hopes and desires of mankind; all the everlasting truths that have been found false; all the eternal faiths discovered to save, until it was discovered they damned. The strange black creature grew and grew till it seemed to fill the room, and Dick and I to be but shadows floating in the air.

I forced from myself a laugh, that only in part, however, broke the spell, and inquired of Dick how he had acquired possession of it.

"It came to me," he answered, "one night six months ago. I was down on my luck at the time. Two of my plays, on which I had built great hopes, had failed, one on top of the other — you remember them — and it appeared absurd to think that any manager would ever look at anything of mine again. Old Walcott had just told me that he did not consider it right of me under all the circumstances to hold Lizzie any longer to her engagement, and that I ought to go away and give her a chance of forgetting me, and I had agreed with him. I was alone in the world, and heavily in debt. Altogether things seemed about as hopeless as they could be, and I don't mind confessing to you now that I had made up my mind to blow out my brains that very evening. I had loaded my revolver, and it lay before me on the desk. My hand was toying with it when I heard a faint scratching at the door. I paid no attention at first, but it grew more persistent, and at length, to stop the faint noise which excited me more than I could account for, I rose and opened the door and *it* walked in.

"It perched itself upon the corner of my desk beside the loaded pistol, and sat there bolt upright looking at me; and I, pushing back my chair, sat looking at it. And there came a letter telling me that a man of whose name I had never heard had been killed by a cow in Melbourne, and that under his will a legacy of three thousand pounds fell into the estate of a distant relative of my own who had died peacefully and utterly insolvent eighteen months previously, leaving me his sole heir and representative, and I put the revolver back into the drawer."

"Do you think Pyramids would come and stop with me for a week?" I asked, reaching over to stroke the cat as it lay softly purring on Dick's knee.

"Maybe he will some day," replied Dick in a low voice, but before the answer came — I know not why — I had regretted the jesting words.

"I came to talk to him as though he were a human creature," continued Dick, "and to discuss things with him. My last play I regard as a collaboration; indeed, it is far more his than mine."

I should have thought Dick mad had not the cat been sitting there before me with its eyes looking into mine. As it was, I only grew more interested in his tale.

"It was rather a cynical play as I first wrote it," he went on, "a truthful picture of a certain corner of society as I saw and knew it. From an artistic point of view I felt it was good; from the box-office standard it was doubtful. I drew it from my desk on the third evening after Pyramids' advent, and read it through. He sat on the arm of the chair and looked over the pages as I turned them.

"It was the best thing I had ever written. Insight into life ran through every line, I found myself reading it again with delight. Suddenly a voice beside me said: —

"'Very clever, my boy, very clever indeed. If you would just turn it topsy-turvy, change all those bitter, truthful speeches into noble sentiments; make your Under-Secretary for Foreign Affairs (who never has been a popular character) die in the last act instead of the Yorkshireman, and let your bad woman be reformed by her love for the hero and go off somewhere by herself and be good to the poor in a black frock, the piece might be worth putting on the stage.'

"I turned indignantly to see who was speaking. The opinions sounded like those of a theatrical manager. No one was in the room but I and the cat. No doubt I had been talking to myself, but the voice was strange to me.

"'Be reformed by her love for the hero!' I retorted, contemptuously, for I was unable to grasp the idea that I was arguing only with myself, 'why it's his mad passion for her that ruins his life.'

"'And will ruin the play with the great B.P.,' returned the other voice. 'The British dramatic hero has no passion, but a pure and respectful admiration for an honest, hearty English girl — pronounced "gey-url." You don't know the canons of your art.'

"'And besides,' I persisted, unheeding the interruption, 'women born and bred and soaked for thirty years in an atmosphere of sin don't reform.'

"'Well, this one's got to, that's all,' was the sneering reply, 'let her hear an organ.'

"'But as an artist -,' I protested.

"'You will be always unsuccessful,' was the rejoinder. 'My dear fellow, you and your plays, artistic or in artistic, will be forgotten in a very few years hence. You give the world what it wants, and the world will give you what you want. Please, if you wish to live.'

"So, with Pyramids beside me day by day, I re-wrote the play, and whenever I felt a thing to be utterly impossible and false I put it down with a grin. And every character I made to talk clap-trap sentiment while Pyramids purred, and I took care that everyone of my puppets did that which was right in the eyes of the lady with the lorgnettes in the second row of the dress circle; and old Hewson says the play will run five hundred nights.

"But what is worst," concluded Dick, "is that I am not ashamed of myself, and that I seem content."

"What do you think the animal is?" I asked with a laugh, "an evil spirit"? For it had passed into the next room and so out through the open window, and its strangely still green eyes no longer drawing mine towards them, I felt my common sense returning to me.

"You have not lived with it for six months," answered Dick quietly, "and felt its eyes for ever on you as I have. And I am not the only one. You know Canon Whycherly, the great preacher?"

"My knowledge of modern church history is not extensive," I replied. "I know him by name, of course. What about him?"

"He was a curate in the East End," continued Dick, "and for ten years he laboured, poor and unknown, leading one of those noble, heroic lives that here and there men do yet live, even in this age. Now he is the prophet of the fashionable up-to-date Christianity of South Kensington, drives to his pulpit behind a pair of thorough-bred Arabs, and his waistcoat is taking to itself the curved line of prosperity. He was in here the other morning on behalf of Princess —-. They are giving a performance of one of my plays in aid of the Destitute Vicars' Fund."

"And did Pyramids discourage him?" I asked, with perhaps the suggestion of a sneer.

"No," answered Dick, "so far as I could judge, it approved the scheme. The point of the matter is that the moment Whycherly came into the room the cat walked over to him and rubbed itself affectionately against his legs. He stood and stroked it."

"'Oh, so it's come to you, has it?' he said, with a curious smile.

"There was no need for any further explanation between us. I understood what lay behind those few words."

I lost sight of Dick for some time, though I heard a good deal of him, for he was rapidly climbing into the position of the most successful dramatist of the day, and Pyramids I had forgotten all about, until one afternoon calling on an artist friend who had lately emerged from the shadows of starving struggle into the sunshine of popularity, I saw a pair of green eyes that seemed familiar to me gleaming at me from a dark corner of the studio.

"Why, surely," I exclaimed, crossing over to examine the animal more closely, "why, yes, you've got Dick Dunkerman's cat."

He raised his face from the easel and glanced across at me.

"Yes," he said, "we can't live on ideals," and I, remembering, hastened to change the conversation.

Since then I have met Pyramids in the rooms of many friends of mine. They give him different names, but I am sure it is the same cat, I know those green eyes. He always brings them luck, but they are never quite the same men again afterwards.

Sometimes I sit wondering if I hear his scratching at the door.

THE MINOR POET'S STORY

"It doesn't suit you at all," I answered.

"You're very disagreeable," said she, "I shan't ever ask your advice again."

"Nobody," I hastened to add, "would look well in it. You, of course, look less awful in it than any other woman would, but it's not your style."

"He means," exclaimed the Minor Poet, "that the thing itself not being pre-eminently beautiful, it does not suit, is not in agreement with you. The contrast between you and anything approaching the ugly or the commonplace, is too glaring to be aught else than displeasing."

"He didn't say it," replied the Woman of the World; "and besides it isn't ugly. It's the very latest fashion."

"Why is it," asked the Philosopher, "that women are such slaves to fashion? They think clothes, they talk clothes, they read clothes, yet they have never understood clothes. The purpose of dress, after the primary object of warmth has been secured, is to adorn, to beautify the particular wearer. Yet not one woman in a thousand stops to consider what colours will go best with her complexion, what cut will best hide the defects or display the advantages of her figure. If it be the fashion, she must wear it. And so we have pale-faced girls looking ghastly in shades suitable to dairy-maids, and dots waddling about in costumes fit and proper to six-footers. It is as if crows insisted on wearing cockatoo's feathers on their heads, and rabbits ran about with peacocks' tails fastened behind them."

"And are not you men every bit as foolish?" retorted the Girton Girl. "Sack coats come into fashion, and dumpy little men trot up and down in them, looking like butter-tubs on legs. You go about in July melting under frock-coats and chimney-pot hats, and because it is the stylish thing to do, you all play tennis in still shirts and stand-up collars, which is idiotic. If fashion decreed that you should play cricket in a pair of top-boots and a diver's helmet, you would play cricket in a pair of top-boots and a diver's helmet, and dub every sensible fellow who didn't a cad. It's worse in you than in us; men are supposed to think for themselves, and to be capable of it, the womanly woman isn't."

"Big women and little men look well in nothing," said the Woman of the World. "Poor Emily was five foot ten and a half, and never looked an inch under seven foot, whatever she wore. Empires came into fashion, and the poor child looked like the giant's baby in a pantomime. We thought the Greek might help her, but it only suggested a Crystal Palace statue tied up in a sheet, and tied up badly; and when puff-sleeves and shoulder-capes were in and Teddy stood up behind her at a water-party and sang 'Under the spreading chestnut-tree,' she took it as a personal insult and boxed his ears. Few men liked to be seen with her, and I'm sure George proposed to her partly with the idea of saving himself the expense of a step-ladder, she reaches down his boots for him from the top shelf."

"I," said the Minor Poet, "take up the position of not wanting to waste my brain upon the subject. Tell me what to wear, and I will wear it, and there is an end of the matter. If Society says, 'Wear blue shirts and white collars,' I wear blue shirts and white collars. If she says, 'The time has now come when hats should be broad-brimmed,' I take unto myself a broad-brimmed hat. The question does not interest me sufficiently for me to argue it. It is your fop who refuses to follow fashion. He wishes to attract attention to himself by being peculiar. A novelist whose books pass unnoticed, gains distinction by designing his own necktie; and many an artist, following the line of least resistance, learns to let his hair grow instead of learning to paint."

"The fact is," remarked the Philosopher, "we are the mere creatures of fashion. Fashion dictates to us our religion, our morality, our affections, our thoughts. In one age successful cattle-lifting is a virtue, a few hundred years later company-promoting takes its place as a respectable and legitimate business. In England and America Christianity is fashionable, in Turkey, Mohammedanism, and 'the crimes of Clapham are chaste in Martaban.' In Japan a woman dresses down to the knees, but would be considered immodest if she displayed bare arms. In Europe it is legs that no pure-minded woman is supposed to possess. In China we worship our mother-in-law and despise our wife; in England we treat our wife with respect, and regard our mother-in-law as the bulwark of comic journalism. The stone age, the iron age, the age of faith, the age of infidelism, the philosophic age, what are they but the passing fashions of the world? It is fashion, fashion, fashion wherever we turn. Fashion waits beside our cradle to lead us by the hand through life. Now literature is sentimental, now hopefully humorous, now psychological, now new-womanly. Yesterday's pictures are the laughing-stock of the up-to-date artist of to-day, and to-day's art will be sneered at to-morrow. Now it is fashionable to be democratic, to pretend that no virtue or wisdom can exist outside corduroy, and to abuse the middle classes. One season we go slumming, and the next we are all socialists. We think we are thinking; we are simply dressing ourselves up in words we do not understand for the gods to laugh at us."

"Don't be pessimistic," retorted the Minor Poet, "pessimism is going out. You call such changes fashions, I call them the footprints of progress. Each phase of thought is an advance upon the former, bringing the footsteps of the many nearer to the landmarks left by the mighty climbers of the past upon the mountain paths of truth. The crowd that was satisfied with *The Derby Day* now appreciates Millet. The public that were content to wag their heads to *The Bohemian Girl* have made Wagner popular."

"And the play lovers, who stood for hours to listen to Shakespeare," interrupted the Philosopher, "now crowd to music-halls."

"The track sometimes descends for a little way, but it will wind upwards again," returned the Poet. "The music-hall itself is improving; I consider it the duty of every intellectual man to visit such places. The mere influence of his presence helps to elevate the tone of the performance. I often go myself!"

"I was looking," said the Woman of the World, "at some old illustrated papers of thirty years ago, showing the men dressed in those very absurd trousers, so extremely roomy about the waist, and so extremely tight about the ankles. I recollect poor papa in them; I always used to long to fill them out by pouring in sawdust at the top."

"You mean the peg-top period," I said. "I remember them distinctly myself, but it cannot be more than three-and-twenty years ago at the outside."

"That is very nice of you," replied the Woman of the World, "and shows more tact than I should have given you credit for. It could, as you say, have been only twenty-three years ago. I know I was a very little girl at the time. I think there must be some subtle connection between clothes and thought. I cannot imagine men in those trousers and Dundreary whiskers talking as you fellows are talking now, any more than I could conceive of a woman in a crinoline and a poke bonnet smoking a cigarette. I think it must be so, because dear mother used to be the most easy-going woman in the world in her ordinary clothes, and would let papa smoke all over the house. But about once every three weeks she would put on a hideous old-fashioned black silk dress, that looked as if Queen Elizabeth must have slept in it during one of those seasons when she used to go about sleeping anywhere, and then we all had to sit up. 'Look out, ma's got her black silk dress on,' came to be a regular formula. We could always make papa take us out for a walk or a drive by whispering it to him."

"I can never bear to look at those pictures of by-gone fashions," said the Old Maid, "I see the by-gone people in them, and it makes me feel as though the faces that we love are only passing fashions with the rest. We wear them for a little while upon our hearts, and think so much of them, and then there comes a time when we lay them by, and forget them, and newer faces take their place, and we are satisfied. It seems so sad."

"I wrote a story some years ago," remarked the Minor Poet, "about a young Swiss guide, who was betrothed to a laughing little French peasant girl."

"Named Suzette," interrupted the Girton Girl. "I know her. Go on."

"Named Jeanne," corrected the Poet, "the majority of laughing French girls, in fiction, are named Suzette, I am well aware. But this girl's mother's family was English. She was christened Jeanne after an aunt Jane, who lived in Birmingham, and from whom she had expectations."

"I beg your pardon," apologised the Girton Girl, "I was not aware of that fact. What happened to her?"

"One morning, a few days before the date fixed for the wedding," said the Minor Poet, "she started off to pay a visit to a relative living in the village, the other side of the mountain. It was a dangerous track, climbing half-way up the mountain before it descended again, and skirting more than one treacherous slope, but the girl was mountain born and bred, sure-footed as a goat, and no one dreamed of harm."

"She went over, of course," said the Philosopher, "those sure-footed girls always do."

"What happened," replied the Minor Poet, "was never known. The girl was never seen again."

"And what became of her lover?" asked the Girton Girl. "Was he, when next year's snow melted, and the young men of the village went forth to gather Edelweiss, wherewith to deck their sweethearts, found by them dead, beside her, at the bottom of the crevasse?"

"No," said the Poet; "you do not know this story, you had better let me tell it. Her lover returned the morning before the wedding day, to be met with the news. He gave way to no sign of grief, he repelled all consolation. Taking his rope and axe he went up into the mountain by himself. All through the winter he haunted the track by which she must have travelled, indifferent to the danger that he ran, impervious apparently to cold, or hunger, or fatigue, undeterred by storm, or mist, or avalanche. At the beginning of the spring he returned to the village, purchased building utensils, and day after day carried them back with him up into the mountain. He hired no labour, he rejected the proffered assistance of his brother guides. Choosing an almost inaccessible spot, at the edge of the great glacier, far from all paths, he built himself a hut, with his own hands; and there for eighteen years he lived alone.

"In the 'season' he earned good fees, being known far and wide as one of the bravest and hardiest of all the guides, but few of his clients liked him, for he was a silent, gloomy man, speaking little, and with never a laugh or jest on the journey. Each fall, having provisioned himself, he would retire to his solitary hut, and bar the door, and no human soul would set eyes on him again until the snows melted.

"One year, however, as the spring days wore on, and he did not appear among the guides, as was his wont, the elder men, who remembered his story and pitied him, grew uneasy; and, after much deliberation, it was determined that a party of them should force their way up to his eyrie. They cut their path across the ice where no foot among them had trodden before, and finding at length the lonely snow-encompassed hut, knocked loudly with their axe-staves on the door; but only the whirling echoes from the glacier's thousand walls replied, so the foremost put his strong shoulder to the worn timber and the door flew open with a crash.

"They found him dead, as they had more than half expected, lying stiff and frozen on the rough couch at the farther end of the hut; and, beside him, looking down upon him with a placid face, as a mother might watch beside her sleeping child, stood Jeanne. She wore the flowers pinned to her dress that she had gathered when their eyes had last seen her. The girl's face that had laughed back to their good-bye in the village, nineteen years ago.

"A strange steely light clung round her, half illuminating, half obscuring her, and the men drew back in fear, thinking they saw a vision, till one, bolder than the rest, stretched out his hand and touched the ice that formed her coffin.

"For eighteen years the man had lived there with this face that he had loved. A faint flush still lingered on the fair cheeks, the laughing lips were still red. Only at one spot, above her temple, the wavy hair lay matted underneath a clot of blood."

The Minor Poet ceased.

"What a very unpleasant way of preserving one's love!" said the Girton Girl.

"When did the story appear?" I asked. "I don't remember reading it."

"I never published it," explained the Minor Poet. "Within the same week two friends of mine, one of whom had just returned from Norway and the other from Switzerland, confided to me their intention of writing stories about girls who had fallen into glaciers, and who had been found by their friends long afterwards, looking as good as new; and a few days later I chanced upon a book, the heroine of which had been dug out of a glacier alive three hundred years after she had fallen in. There seemed to be a run on ice maidens, and I decided not to add to their number."

"It is curious," said the Philosopher, "how there seems to be a fashion even in thought. An idea has often occurred to me that has seemed to me quite new, and taking up a newspaper I have found that some man in Russia or San Francisco has just been saying the very same thing in almost the very same words. We say a thing is 'in the air'; it is more true than we are aware of. Thought does not grow in us. It is a thing apart, we simply gather it. All truths, all discoveries, all inventions, they have not come to us from any one man. The time grows ripe for them, and from this corner of the earth and from that, hands, guided by some instinct, grope for and grasp them. Buddha and Christ seize hold of the morality needful to civilisation, and promulgate it, unknown to one another, the one on the shores of the Ganges, the other by the Jordan. A dozen forgotten explorers, *feeling* America, prepared the way for Columbus to discover it. A deluge of blood is required to sweep away old follies, and Rousseau and Voltaire, and a myriad others are set to work to fashion the storm clouds. The steam-engine, the spinning loom is 'in the air.' A thousand brains are busy with them, a few go further than the rest. It is idle to talk of human thought; there is no such thing. Our minds are fed as our bodies with the food God has provided for us. Thought hangs by the wayside, and we pick it and cook it, and eat it, and cry out what clever 'thinkers' we are!"

"I cannot agree with you," replied the Minor Poet, "if we were simply automata, as your argument would suggest, what was the purpose of creating us?"

"The intelligent portion of mankind has been asking itself that question for many ages," returned the Philosopher.

"I hate people who always think as I do," said the Girton Girl; "there was a girl in our corridor who never would disagree with me. Every opinion I expressed turned out to be her opinion also. It always irritated me."

"That might have been weak-mindedness," said the Old Maid, which sounded ambiguous.

"It is not so unpleasant as having a person always disagreeing with you," said the Woman of the World. "My cousin Susan never would agree with any one. If I came down in red she would say, 'Why don't you try green, dear? every one says you look so well in green'; and when I wore green she would say, 'Why have you given up red dear? I thought you rather fancied yourself in red.' When I told her of my engagement to Tom, she burst into tears and said she couldn't help it. She had always felt that George and I were intended for one another; and when Tom never wrote for two whole months, and behaved disgracefully in — in other ways, and I told her I was engaged to George, she reminded me of every word I had ever said about my affection for Tom, and of how I had ridiculed poor George. Papa used to say, 'If any man ever tells Susan that he loves her, she will argue him out of it, and will never accept him until he has jilted her, and will refuse to marry him every time he asks her to fix the day.'"

"Is she married?" asked the Philosopher.

"Oh, yes," answered the Woman of the World, "and is devoted to her children. She lets them do everything they don't want to."

THE DEGENERATION
OF THOMAS HENRY

The most respectable cat I have ever known was Thomas Henry. His original name was Thomas, but it seemed absurd to call him that. The family at Hawarden would as soon think of addressing Mr. Gladstone as "Bill." He came to us from the Reform Club, *viâ* the butcher, and the moment I saw him I felt that of all the clubs in London that was the club he must have come from. Its atmosphere of solid dignity and petrified conservatism seemed to cling to him. Why he left the club I am unable, at this distance of time, to remember positively, but I am inclined to think that it came about owing to a difference with the new *chef*, an overbearing personage who wanted all the fire to himself. The butcher, hearing of the quarrel, and knowing us as a catless family, suggested a way out of the *impasse* that was welcomed both by cat and cook. The parting between them, I believe, was purely formal, and Thomas arrived prejudiced in our favour.

My wife, the moment she saw him, suggested Henry as a more suitable name. It struck me that the combination of the two would be still more appropriate, and accordingly, in the privacy of the domestic circle, Thomas Henry he was called. When speaking of him to friends, we generally alluded to him as Thomas Henry, Esquire.

He approved of us in his quiet, undemonstrative way. He chose my own particular easy chair for himself, and stuck to it. An ordinary cat I should have shot out, but Thomas Henry was not the cat one chivvies. Had I made it clear to him that I objected to his presence in my chair, I feel convinced he would have regarded me much as I should expect to be regarded by Queen Victoria, were that gracious Lady to call upon me in a friendly way, and were I to inform her that I was busy, and request her to look in again some other afternoon. He would have risen, and have walked away, but he never would have spoken to me again so long as we lived under the same roof.

We had a lady staying with us at the time — she still resides with us, but she is now older, and possessed of more judgment — who was no respecter of cats. Her argument was that seeing the tail stuck up, and came conveniently to one's hand, that was the natural appendage by which to raise a cat. She also laboured under the error that the way to feed a cat was to ram things into its head, and that its pleasure was to be taken out for a ride in a doll's perambulator. I dreaded the first meeting of Thomas Henry with this lady. I feared lest she should give him a false impression of us as a family, and that we should suffer in his eyes.

But I might have saved myself all anxiety. There was a something about Thomas Henry that checked forwardness and damped familiarity. His attitude towards her was friendly but firm. Hesitatingly, and with a new-born respect for cats, she put out her hand timidly towards its tail. He gently put it on the other side, and looked at her. It was not an angry look nor an offended look. It was the expression with which Solomon might have received the advances of the Queen of Sheba. It expressed condescension, combined with distance.

He was really a most gentlemanly cat. A friend of mine, who believes in the doctrine of the transmigration of souls, was convinced that he was Lord Chesterfield. He never clamoured for food, as other cats do. He would sit beside me at meals, and wait till he was served. He would eat only the knuckle-end of a leg of mutton, and would never look at over-done beef. A visitor of ours once offered him a piece of gristle; he said nothing, but quietly left the room, and we did not see him again until our friend had departed.

But every one has his price, and Thomas Henry's price was roast duck. Thomas Henry's attitude in the presence of roast duck came to me as a psychological revelation. It showed me at once the lower and more animal side of his nature. In the presence of roast duck Thomas Henry became simply and merely a cat, swayed by all the savage instincts of his race. His dignity fell from him as a cloak. He clawed for roast duck, he grovelled for it. I believe he would have sold himself to the devil for roast duck.

We accordingly avoided that particular dish: it was painful to see a cat's character so completely demoralised. Besides, his manners, when roast duck was on the table, afforded a bad example to the children.

He was a shining light among all the cats of our neighbourhood. One might have set one's watch by his movements. After dinner he invariably took half an hour's constitutional in the square; at ten o'clock each night, precisely, he returned to the area door, and at eleven o'clock he was asleep in my easy chair. He made no friends among the other cats. He took no pleasure in fighting, and I doubt his ever having loved, even in youth; his was too cold and self-contained a nature, female society he regarded with utter indifference.

So he lived with us a blameless existence during the whole winter. In the summer we took him down with us into the country.

We thought the change of air would do him good; he was getting decidedly stout. Alas, poor Thomas Henry! the country was his ruin. What brought about the change I cannot say: maybe the air was too bracing. He slid down the moral incline with frightful rapidity. The first night he stopped out till eleven, the second night he never came home at all, the third night he came home at six o'clock in the morning, minus half the fur on the top of his head. Of course, there was a lady in the case, indeed, judging by the riot that went on all night, I am inclined to think there must have been a dozen. He was certainly a fine cat, and they took to calling for him in the day time. Then gentleman cats who had been wronged took to calling also, and demanding explanations, which Thomas Henry, to do him justice, was always ready to accord.

The village boys used to loiter round all day to watch the fights, and angry housewives would be constantly charging into our kitchen to fling dead cats upon the table, and appeal to Heaven and myself for justice. Our kitchen became a veritable cat's morgue, and I had to purchase a new kitchen table. The cook said it would make her work simpler if she could keep a table entirely to herself. She said it quite confused her, having so many dead cats lying round among her joints and vegetables: she was afraid of making a mistake. Accordingly, the old table was placed under the window, and devoted to the cats; and, after that, she would never allow anyone to bring a cat, however dead, to her table.

"What do you want me to do with it," I heard her asking an excited lady on one occasion; "cook it?"

"It's my cat," said the lady; "that's what that is."

"Well, I'm not making cat pie to-day," answered our cook. "You take it to its proper table. This is my table."

At first, "Justice" was generally satisfied with half a crown, but as time went on cats rose. I had hitherto regarded cats as a cheap commodity, and I became surprised at the value attached to them. I began to think seriously of breeding cats as an industry. At the prices current in that village, I could have made an income of thousands.

"Look what your beast has done," said one irate female, to whom I had been called out in the middle of dinner.

I looked. Thomas Henry appeared to have "done" a mangy, emaciated animal, that must have been far happier dead than alive. Had the poor creature been mine I should have thanked him; but some people never know when they are well off.

"I wouldn't ha' taken a five-pun' note for that cat," said the lady.

"It's a matter of opinion," I replied, "but personally I think you would have been unwise to refuse it. Taking the animal as it stands, I don't feel inclined to give you more than a shilling for it. If you think you can do better by taking it elsewhere, you do so."

"He was more like a Christian than a cat," said the lady.

"I'm not taking dead Christians," I answered firmly, "and even if I were I wouldn't give more than a shilling for a specimen like that. You can consider him as a Christian, or you can consider him as a cat; but he's not worth more than a shilling in either case."

We settled eventually for eighteenpence.

The number of cats that Thomas Henry contrived to dispose of also surprised me. Quite a massacre of cats seemed to be in progress.

One evening, going into the kitchen, for I made it a practice now to visit the kitchen each evening, to inspect the daily consignment of dead cats, I found, among others, a curiously marked tortoiseshell cat, lying on the table.

"That cat's worth half a sovereign," said the owner, who was standing by, drinking beer.

I took up the animal, and examined it.

"Your cat killed him yesterday," continued the man. "It's a burning shame."

"My cat has killed him three times," I replied. "He was killed on Saturday as Mrs. Hedger's cat; on Monday he was killed for Mrs. Myers. I was not quite positive on Monday; but I had my suspicions, and I made notes. Now I recognise him. You take my advice, and bury him before he breeds a fever. I don't care how many lives a cat has got; I only pay for one."

We gave Thomas Henry every chance to reform; but he only went from bad to worse, and added poaching and chicken-stalking to his other crimes, and I grew tired of paying for his vices.

I consulted the gardener, and the gardener said he had known cats taken that way before.

"Do you know of any cure for it?" I asked.

"Well, sir," replied the gardener, "I have heard as how a dose of brickbat and pond is a good thing in a general way."

"We'll try him with a dose just before bed time," I answered. The gardener administered it, and we had no further trouble with him.

Poor Thomas Henry! It shows to one how a reputation for respectability may lie in the mere absence of temptation. Born and bred in the atmosphere of the Reform Club, what gentleman could go wrong? I was sorry for Thomas Henry, and I have never believed in the moral influence of the country since.

THE CITY OF THE SEA

They say, the chroniclers who have written the history of that low-lying, wind-swept coast, that years ago the foam fringe of the ocean lay further to the east; so that where now the North Sea creeps among the treacherous sand-reefs, it was once dry land. In those days, between the Abbey and the sea, there stood a town of seven towers and four rich churches, surrounded by a wall of twelve stones' thickness, making it, as men reckoned then, a place of strength and much import; and the monks, glancing their eyes downward from the Abbey garden on the hill, saw beneath their feet its narrow streets, gay with the ever passing of rich merchandise, saw its many wharves and water-ways, ever noisy with the babel of strange tongues, saw its many painted masts, wagging their grave heads above the dormer roofs and quaintly-carved oak gables.

Thus the town prospered till there came a night when it did evil in the sight of God and man. Those were troublous times to Saxon dwellers by the sea, for the Danish water-rats swarmed round each river mouth, scenting treasure from afar; and by none was the white flash of their sharp, strong teeth more often seen than by the men of Eastern Anglia, and by none in Eastern Anglia more often than by the watchers on the walls of the town of seven towers that once stood upon the dry land, but which now lies twenty fathom deep below the waters. Many a bloody fight raged now without and now within its wall of twelve stones' thickness. Many a groan of dying man, many a shriek of murdered woman, many a wail of mangled child, knocked at the Abbey door upon its way to Heaven, calling the trembling-monks from their beds, to pray for the souls that were passing by.

But at length peace came to the long-troubled land: Dane and Saxon agreeing to dwell in friendship side by side, East Anglia being wide, and there being room for both. And all men rejoiced greatly, for all were weary of a strife in which little had been gained on either side beyond hard blows, and their thoughts were of the ingle-nook. So the long-bearded Danes, their thirsty axes harmless on their backs, passed to and fro in straggling bands, seeking where undisturbed and undisturbing they might build their homes; and thus it came about that Haafager and his company, as the sun was going down, drew near to the town of seven towers, that in those days stood on dry land between the Abbey and the sea.

And the men of the town, seeing the Danes, opened wide their gates saying: —

"We have fought, but now there is peace. Enter, and make merry with us, and to-morrow go your way."

But Haafager made answer: —

"I am an old man, I pray you do not take my words amiss. There is peace between us, as you say, and we thank you for your courtesy, but the stains are still fresh upon our swords. Let us camp here without your walls, and a little later, when the grass has grown upon the fields where we have striven, and our young men have had time to forget, we will make merry together, as men should who dwell side by side in the same land."

But the men of the town still urged Haafager, calling his people neighbours; and the Abbot, who had hastened down, fearing there might be strife, added his words to theirs, saying: —

"Pass in, my children. Let there indeed be peace between you, that the blessing of God may be upon the land, and upon both Dane and Saxon"; for the Abbot saw that the townsmen were well disposed towards the Danes, and knew that men, when they have feasted and drunk together, think kinder of one another.

Then answered Haafager, who knew the Abbot for a holy man: —

"Hold up your staff, my father, that the shadow of the cross your people worship may fall upon our path, so we will pass into the town and there shall be peace between us, for though your gods are not our gods, faith between man and man is of all altars."

And the Abbot held his staff aloft between Haafager's people and the sun, it being fashioned in the form of a cross, and under its shadow the Danes passed by into the town of seven towers, there being of them, with the women and the children, nearly two thousand souls, and the gates were made fast behind them.

So they who had fought face to face, feasted side by side, pledging one another in the wine cup, as was the custom; and Haafager's men, knowing themselves amongst friends, cast aside their arms, and when the feast was done, being weary, they lay down to sleep.

Then an evil voice arose in the town, and said: "Who are these that have come among us to share our land? Are not the stones of our streets red with the blood of wife and child that they have slain? Do men let the wolf go free when they have trapped him with meat? Let us fall upon them now that they are heavy with food and wine, so that not one of them shall escape. Thus no further harm shall come to us from them nor from their children."

And the voice of evil prevailed, and the men of the town of

seven towers fell upon the Danes with whom they had broken meat, even to the women and the little children; and the blood of the people of Haafager cried with a loud voice at the Abbey door, through the long night it cried, saying: —

"I trusted in your spoken word. I broke meat with you. I put my faith in you and in your God. I passed beneath the shadow of your cross to enter your doors. Let your God make answer!"

Nor was there silence till the dawn.

Then the Abbot rose from where he knelt and called to God, saying: —

"Thou hast heard, O God. Make answer."

And there came a great sound from the sea as though a tongue had been given to the deep, so that the monks fell upon their knees in fear; but the Abbot answered: —

"It is the voice of God speaking through the waters. He hath made answer."

And that winter a mighty storm arose, the like of which no man had known before; for the sea was piled upon the dry land until the highest tower of the town of seven towers was not more high; and the waters moved forward over the dry land. And the men of the town of seven towers fled from the oncoming of the waters, but the waters overtook them so that not one of them escaped. And the town of the seven towers and of the four churches, and of the many streets and quays, was buried underneath the waters, and the feet of the waters still moved till they came to the hill whereon the Abbey stood. Then the Abbot prayed to God that the waters might be stayed, and God heard, and the sea came no farther.

And that this tale is true, and not a fable made by the weavers of words, he who doubts may know from the fisher-folk, who to-day ply their calling amongst the reefs and sandbanks of that lonely coast. For there are those among them who, peering from the bows of their small craft, have seen far down beneath their keels a city of strange streets and many quays. But as to this, I, who repeat these things to you, cannot speak of my own knowledge, for this city of the sea is only visible when a rare wind, blowing from the north, sweeps the shadows from the waves; and though on many a sunny day I have drifted where its seven towers should once have stood, yet for me that wind has never blown, pushing back the curtains of the sea, and, therefore, I have strained my eyes in vain.

But this I do know, that the rumbling stones of that ancient Abbey, between which and the foam fringe of the ocean the town of seven towers once lay, now stand upon a wave-washed cliff, and that he who looks forth from its shattered mullions to-day sees only the marshland and the wrinkled waters, hears only the plaint of the circling gulls and the weary crying of the sea.

And that God's anger is not everlasting, and that the evil that there is in men shall be blotted out, he who doubts may also learn from the wisdom of the simple fisher-folk, who dwell about the borders of the marsh-land; for they will tell him that on stormy nights there speaks a deep voice from the sea, calling the dead monks to rise from their forgotten graves, and chant a mass for the souls of the men of the town of seven towers. Clothed in long glittering white, they move with slowly pacing feet around the Abbey's grass-grown aisles, and the music of their prayers is heard above the screaming of the storm. And to this I also can bear witness, for I have seen the passing of their shrouded forms behind the blackness of the shattered shafts; I have heard their sweet, sad singing above the wailing of the wind.

Thus for many ages have the dead monks prayed that the men of the town of seven towers may be forgiven. Thus, for many ages yet shall they so pray, till the day come when of their once fair Abbey not a single stone shall stand upon its fellow; and in that day it shall be known that the anger of God against the men of the town of seven towers has passed away; and in that day the feet of the waters shall move back, and the town of seven towers shall stand again upon the dry land.

There be some, I know, who say that this is but a legend; who will tell you that the shadowy shapes that you may see with your own eyes on stormy nights, waving their gleaming arms behind the ruined buttresses are but of phosphorescent foam, tossed by the raging waves above the cliffs; and that the sweet, sad harmony cleaving the trouble of the night is but the æolian music of the wind.

But such are of the blind, who see only with their eyes. For myself I see the white-robed monks, and hear the chanting of their mass for the souls of the sinful men of the town of seven towers. For it has been said that when an evil deed is done, a prayer is born to follow it through time into eternity, and plead for it. Thus is the whole world clasped around with folded hands both of the dead and of the living, as with a shield, lest the shafts of God's anger should consume it.

Therefore, I know that the good monks of this nameless Abbey are still praying that the sin of those they love may be forgiven.

God grant good men may say a mass for us.

DRIFTWOOD

CHARACTERS

MR. TRAVERS.

MRS. TRAVERS.

MARION [their daughter].

DAN [a gentleman of no position].

* * * * *

SCENE: A room opening upon a garden. The shadows creep from their corners, driving before them the fading twilight.

MRS. TRAVERS sits in a wickerwork easy chair. MR. TRAVERS, smoking a cigar, sits the other side of the room. MARION stands by the open French window, looking out.

MR. TRAVERS. Nice little place Harry's got down here.

MRS. TRAVERS. Yes; I should keep this on if I were you, Marion. You'll find it very handy. One can entertain so cheaply up the river; one is not expected to make much of a show. [She turns to her husband.] Your poor cousin Emily used to work off quite half her list that way — relations and Americans, and those sort of people, you know — at that little place of theirs at Goring. You remember it — a poky hole I always thought it, but it had a lot of green stuff over the door — looked very pretty from the other side of the river. She always used to have cold meat and pickles for lunch — called it a picnic. People said it was so homely and simple.

MR. TRAVERS. They didn't stop long, I remember.

MRS. TRAVERS. And there was a special champagne she always kept for the river — only twenty-five shillings a dozen, I think she told me she paid for it, and very good it was too, for the price. That old Indian major — what was his name? — said it suited him better than anything else he had ever tried. He always used to drink a tumblerful before breakfast; such a funny thing to do. I've often wondered where she got it.

MR. TRAVERS. So did most people who tasted it. Marion wants to forget those lessons, not learn them. She is going to marry a rich man who will be able to entertain his guests decently.

MRS. TRAVERS. Oh, well, James, I don't know. None of us can afford to live up to the income we want people to think we've got.

One must economise somewhere. A pretty figure we should cut in the county if I didn't know how to make fivepence look like a shilling. And, besides, there are certain people that one has to be civil to, that, at the same time, one doesn't want to introduce into one's regular circle. If you take my advice, Marion, you won't encourage those sisters of Harry's more than you can help. They're dear sweet girls, and you can be very nice to them; but don't have them too much about. Their manners are terribly old-fashioned, and they've no notion how to dress, and those sort of people let down the tone of a house.

MARION. I'm not likely to have many "dear sweet girls" on my visiting list. [With a laugh.] There will hardly be enough in common to make the company desired, on either side.

MRS. TRAVERS. Well, I only want you to be careful, my dear. So much depends on how you begin, and with prudence there's really no reason why you shouldn't do very well. I suppose there's no doubt about Harry's income. He won't object to a few inquiries?

MARION. I think you may trust me to see to that, mamma. It would be a bad bargain for me, if even the cash were not certain.

MR. TRAVERS [jumping up]. Oh, I do wish you women wouldn't discuss the matter in that horribly business-like way. One would think the girl was selling herself.

MRS. TRAVERS. Oh, don't be foolish, James. One must look at the practical side of these things. Marriage is a matter of sentiment to a man — very proper that it should be. A woman has to remember that she's fixing her position for life.

MARION. You see, papa dear, it's her one venture. If she doesn't sell herself to advantage then, she doesn't get another opportunity — very easily.

MR. TRAVERS. Umph! When I was a young man, girls talked more about love and less about income.

MARION. Perhaps they had not our educational advantages.

[DAN enters from the garden. He is a man of a little over forty, his linen somewhat frayed about the edges.]

MRS. TRAVERS. Ah! We were just wondering where all you people had got to.

DAN. We've been out sailing. I've been sent up to fetch you. It's delightful on the river. The moon is just rising.

MRS. TRAVERS. But it's so cold.

MR. TRAVERS. Oh, never mind the cold. It's many a long year since you and I looked at the moon together. It will do us good.

MRS. TRAVERS. Ah, dear. Boys will be boys. Give me my wrap then.

[DAN places it about her. They move towards the window, where they stand talking. MARION has slipped out and returns with her father's cap. He takes her face between his hands and looks at her.]

MR. TRAVERS. Do you really care for Harry, Marion?

MARION. As much as one can care for a man with five thousand a year. Perhaps he will make it ten one day — then I shall care for him twice as much. [Laughs.]

MR. TRAVERS. And are you content with this marriage?

MARION. Quite.

[He shakes his head gravely at her.]

MRS. TRAVERS. Aren't you coming, Marion?

MARION. No. I'm feeling tired.

[MR. and MRS. TRAVERS go out.]

DAN. Are you going to leave Harry alone with two pairs of lovers?

MARION [with a laugh]. Yes — let him see how ridiculous they look. I hate the night — it follows you and asks questions. Shut it out. Come and talk to me. Amuse me.

DAN. What shall I talk to you about?

MARION. Oh, tell me all the news. What is the world doing? Who has run away with whose wife? Who has been swindling whom? Which philanthropist has been robbing the poor? What saint has been discovered sinning? What is the latest scandal? Who has been found out? and what is it they have been doing? and what is everybody saying about it?

DAN. Would it amuse you?

MARION [she sits by the piano, softly touching the keys, idly recalling many memories]. What should it do? Make me weep? Should not one be glad to know one's friends better?

DAN. I wish you wouldn't be clever. Everyone one meets is

clever nowadays. It came in when the sun-flower went out. I preferred the sun-flower; it was more amusing.

MARION. And stupid people, I suppose, will come in when the clever people go out. I prefer the clever. They have better manners. You're exceedingly disagreeable. [She leaves the piano, and, throwing herself upon the couch, takes up a book.]

DAN. I know I am. The night has been with me also. It follows one and asks questions.

MARION. What questions has it been asking you?

DAN. Many — and so many of them have no answer. Why am I a useless, drifting log upon the world's tide? Why have all the young men passed me? Why am I, at thirty-nine, let us say, with brain, with power, with strength — nobody thinks I am worth anything, but I am — I know it. I might have been an able editor, devoting every morning from ten till three to arranging the affairs of the Universe, or a popular politician, trying to understand what I was talking about, and to believe it. And what am I? A newspaper reporter, at three-ha'pence a line — I beg their pardon, its occasionally twopence.

MARION. Does it matter?

DAN. Does it matter! Does it matter whether a Union Jack or a Tricolor floats over the turrets of Badajoz? yet we pour our blood into its ditches to decide the argument. Does it matter whether one star more or less is marked upon our charts? yet we grow blind peering into their depths. Does it matter that one keel should slip through the grip of the Polar ice? yet nearer, nearer to it, we pile our whitening bones. And it's worth playing, the game of life. And there's a meaning in it. It's worth playing, if only that it strengthens the muscles of our souls. I'd like to have taken a hand in it.

MARION. Why didn't you?

DAN. No partner. Dull playing by oneself. No object.

MARION [after a silence]. What was she like?

DAN. So like you that there are times when I almost wish I had never met you. You set me thinking about myself, and that is a subject I find it pleasanter to forget.

MARION. And this woman that was like me — she could have made a man's life?

DAN. Ay!

MARION. Won't you tell me about her? Had she many faults?

DAN. Enough to love her by.

MARION. But she must have been good.

DAN. Good enough to be a woman.

MARION. That might mean so much or so little.

DAN. It should mean much to my thinking. There are few women.

MARION. Few! I thought the economists held that there were too many of us.

DAN. Not enough — not enough to go round. That is why a true woman has many lovers.

[There is a silence between them. Then MARION rises, but their eyes do not meet.]

MARION. How serious we have grown!

DAN. They say a dialogue between a man and woman always does.

MARION [she moves away, then, hesitating, half returns]. May I ask you a question?

DAN. That is an easy favour to grant.

MARION. If — if at any time you felt regard again for a woman, would you, for her sake, if she wished it, seek to gain, even now, that position in the world which is your right — which would make her proud of your friendship — would make her feel that even her life had not been altogether without purpose?

DAN. Too late! The old hack can only look over the hedge, and watch the field race by. The old ambition stirs within me at times — especially after a glass of good wine — and Harry's wine — God bless him — is excellent — but to-morrow morning — [with a shrug of his shoulders he finishes his meaning].

MARION. Then she could do nothing?

DAN. Nothing for his fortunes — much for himself. My dear young lady, never waste pity on a man in love — nor upon a child crying for the moon. The moon is a good thing to cry for.

MARION. I am glad I am like her. I am glad that I have met you.

[She gives him her hand, and for a moment he holds it. Then she goes out.]

[A flower has fallen from her breast, whether by chance or meaning, he knows not. He picks it up and kisses it; stands twirling it, undecided for a second, then lets it fall again upon the floor.]

THE END

www.ingramcontent.com/pod-product-compliance
Lightning Source LLC
Chambersburg PA
CBHW020138180626
46810CB00004B/1622